D0765501

FLYIN' SOLO

Also by Peggy O'Neal Peden

A Nashville mystery

YOUR KILLIN' HEART
GONE MISSIN' *

* available from Severn House

FLYIN' SOLO

Peggy O'Neal Peden

**SEVERN
HOUSE**

First world edition published in Great Britain and the USA in 2022
by Severn House, an imprint of Canongate Books Ltd,
14 High Street, Edinburgh EH1 1TE.

Trade paperback edition first published in Great Britain and the USA in 2022
by Severn House, an imprint of Canongate Books Ltd.

severnhouse.com

British Library Cataloguing-in-Publication Data
A CIP catalogue record for this title is available from the British Library.

ISBN-13: 978-0-7278-5094-2 (cased)
ISBN-13: 978-1-4483-0693-0 (trade paper)
ISBN-13: 978-1-4483-0692-3 (e-book)

All Severn House titles are printed on acid-free paper.

Typeset by Palimpsest Book Production Ltd.,
Falkirk, Stirlingshire, Scotland.
Printed and bound in Great Britain by
TJ Books, Padstow, Cornwall.

To Frances
And to the nurses, doctors, hospital staff, pharmacists,
grocery workers, truck drivers, maintenance workers, lab technicians,
first responders, scientists and waiters who have worked to take care
of us and keep us fed.

ONE

Do you remember . . .
The touch of my hand . . .
The feel of my lips . . .
Your head on my shoulder . . .
The surf on the sand . . .
Do you remember?

Do you remember . . .
The stars in the sky . . .
Our dreams for tomorrow . . .
A faith in forever . . .
The night's last goodbye . . .
Do you remember?

Do you remember . . .
The look in my eyes . . .
Your body next to mine . . .
The future we dreamed . . .
The sound of a sigh . . .

Do you remember? Do you remember . . .
A soft, warm, summer night . . .
My fingers in your hair . . .
Moonlight on the water . . .
The stars above so bright . . .
Do you remember?

Stick Anderson

f Sam Davis had gone with me to my high school reunion, things might have turned out differently. But Sam, my friend and occasional date, maybe more than occasional, is a detective with the Metropolitan Nashville Police Department Homicide Division, and there was a murder that late June weekend.

'I'm sorry, Campbell,' he said, but he didn't sound too sorry. 'I can't go. I don't know when I'll get loose.' Some people will do anything to get out of dressing up and spending the best part of thirty or so hours with strangers. So I went alone.

'You won't be alone,' my friend Barbara insisted. 'You'll be with us.' Us. Us Five, a high school singing group of five with a little more musical talent than originality in choosing a name. Barbara went on to play guitar and sing in college coffee shops. Melinda and her husband were part of a band for the first few years after graduation, and Melinda still plays piano and organ at her church and for weddings. Pam and Betty sing in church choirs. I sing in the shower. I was the only one of Us Five without a husband, but I knew they'd do their best to see that I didn't feel like a ninth wheel.

The reunion was in Adamson's Fork, Tennessee, my hometown, just five miles or so from the county line that now marks the boundary of Metropolitan Nashville. When I was in high school in Adamson's Fork, Nashville was the big city, far enough away that a date in Nashville was a big deal. Driving in Nashville was very different from driving in Adamson's Fork, and teenagers weren't allowed to drive there until we had some experience. A shopping trip to Nashville was a trip. Now, with the interstate highways feeding into the center of the city, Adamson's Fork isn't a small town anymore. It's a bedroom community. Back then, it was a different world.

And this reunion couldn't be worse than the last one. Ten years ago, at our tenth-year reunion, I had even then been the only single one of Us Five. Barbara and Melinda had decided to pair me up with Jeb, also in our class and newly single because his wife had died in a car accident a couple of years before. It didn't seem like a completely bad idea to me.

I had always liked Jeb; he was a nice guy when we were in school; we'd been friends. This reunion didn't have to be the romance of our lifetimes. I thought my expectations were low enough, but, like so many times before, I was wrong.

Jeb was still a nice guy, and part of our reunion that year was at his place, a farm outside of town with a creek running through it, a swing in the shade of a tree, a barn cleaner than my kitchen and, of course, a dog. A friendly dog like one that might have followed Opie home for Aunt Bea to feed. The whole scene was perfect, idyllic, and my friends thought I belonged in that picture.

TWO

Just an ordinary small town boy
With dreams of a big, wide world
Just an ordinary small town boy
In love with a small town girl

Stick Anderson

We met at Jeb's for breakfast on Saturday, and I helped set things up. Melinda had made sure I was on that committee. I was there early, and Jeb and I were both working hard at reconnecting. It just didn't happen. I'm a travel agent. I manage a Hillsboro Village travel agency, in Nashville, in fact. All day, every day I make it easy for people to get out of town. Jeb hated to travel, thought it was overrated, pretentious and too expensive. Besides that, he was afraid to fly. Not that he blamed me for that, of course. Jeb hunted. A lot. And he was apparently good at it. His decorating theme was dead animals. Deer, turkeys, foxes. Everywhere I looked, dead animals looked back. And I get squeamish about picking my own lobster in a restaurant. It was that kind of weekend.

By the end of the dance at a nearby country club that evening, we had exhausted just about every potential common interest. Incredibly enough, we still liked each other; we just didn't like the same things: books, movies, food, sports teams, you name it. I suppose I should have felt flattered that my friends thought all I had to do was show some interest in a man to attract him, but it felt more like it was my fault once again.

'I really don't think he's attracted to me,' I said to Barbara in the ladies' room toward the end of the evening.

'Don't be so picky,' she said. 'He's a very nice man. You need to date a nice man for a change.'

What could I say? Of course, he was a nice man. It had taken me some time, but I had finally realized that it was possible for a man to be nice, attractive, not a menace to society, even liked by children and dogs, and still not be attracted to me.

I heard two months later that Jeb was engaged to another girl from our class. When had that happened? The worst thing was that they hadn't even called me to book their Mediterranean cruise honeymoon.

So I went to this reunion without a date, and there was an extra place at our table for ten at the barbecue Friday night. The barbecue was at Skunk's parents' house, the scene of too many parties in the old days that way too few of my classmates remembered clearly. Old-fashioned, outdoor, colored Christmas lights were strung from the back porch to the unattached garage, lighting up a long table of food and rows of picnic tables. There were coolers of soft drinks, sweating in the melting ice, and kegs of beer.

I happened to be at the end of the driveway reattaching a bunch of balloons to a sign tacked to the mailbox post when a county deputy sheriff pulled up, lights flashing. Busted, I thought. But none of us were underage this time. The deputy opened the trunk of his patrol car and handed over a large glass jug of moonshine to a waiting classmate. A city councilman. I swear. You've got to love a hometown where things like that can still happen once in a while.

I was back in the safety of lights and food, sitting with my friends just one table over from Jeb and his bride, and I had just taken a huge bite of a barbecue sandwich when Fly Young walked up. He was juggling a paper plate of food, a dessert plate, and a soft drink. 'Anybody sitting here? Mind if I join you?'

I nodded while my friends begged him to sit. It was a good thing my mouth was full; otherwise, I'd have been speechless – without an excuse.

Fly Young, born Franklin Lawrence Young, III, had been Fly since the first time he threw a football and it took flight. Knowing adolescent boys, there may have been some zipper humor involved, too, but that never made it out of the locker room. Fly was my first love, and he had broken my heart.

I had been seventeen, and I have never hurt as much since as I did the night I found out that the boy I was in love with, the boy I'd been going steady with for two years, had been seeing someone else, too. A new girl I barely knew. For three weeks. I was clueless, hadn't even known enough to feel threatened.

He was on the football field, and I had just finished a cheer, little bits of my giant chrysanthemum corsage raining gold on the ground around me, when his best friend walked by and told me Fly wouldn't be taking me home after the game. And why. He said he'd give me a ride if I needed one, but I had too much pride for that. I'd have walked first. I cried until sometime after three in the morning.

I got over it, of course. I mean, I was only seventeen years old. But it was the first time my heart had been broken, and nothing hurts like the first time. Fly hadn't been to any previous reunions, so this was the first time I had seen him since high school. I'd like to say his life had been a miserable failure, that dumping me had been the kind of life-defining choice that had foretold the tragic ruin his life would be. Instead he had become a software millionaire, known as Franklin now, not Fly. He'd spent a decade away from Middle Tennessee, then come back to Nashville to found a healthcare software company that dominated the industry. There is no justice.

'Campbell, you look better than ever! Why was it you broke my heart?'

I managed not to choke on my barbecue. 'Hey, Fly.' There were hellos and you-haven't-changed-a-bits with appropriate embarrassed laughter all around. Fly was introduced to the husbands who didn't already know him. Occupations and children were reviewed with self-conscious modesty. These were nice guys, good friends. If I had to be a ninth wheel, this was the best truck to be on.

'What about you, Fly? Your wife isn't with you?' Melinda asked. It was a question you had to be careful about these days, but Fly was a fairly public figure. He and his wife were in the Nashville paper often, sometimes in the business section, sometimes in Living, glittering at a charity benefit. I'm in pretty good shape, good hair, blonde. I don't have to feel embarrassed at the beach, and men still notice when I walk into a room. But she was gorgeous. Long, blonde hair, thin, dramatic cheekbones. Not even my best friends could ask what he saw in her. And she was a rich businesswoman herself. She had started with a diet/exercise plan, which had become a book, *Erika Young's Lifestyle Balance*, which had become a corporation, which had become a financial conglomerate. Her photo stared back from every bookstore window display, every airport book kiosk.

'No, no. Erika couldn't make it.' He was silent a moment. 'Well, hey, I'm among friends, aren't I?' he asked, suddenly solemn. 'We're separating.'

'I'm sorry,' Melinda began. 'I . . .' The rest of us joined in, but Fly shook off the sympathy.

'No. Thanks, but it's been coming for years. We just didn't want to admit it, for the kids' sake, you know.' Fly and Erika had two children, a girl and a boy, both teenagers, both star athletes, both good-looking, both in expensive private schools. I didn't even have a cat. 'When it finally happens, you take a look at your life, you know' – Fly looked at me, then back to the group – 'think about the choices you've made, what's really important. Take stock. It'll be OK. I'm just concerned about the kids. How to make sure they're not hurt by this.' And how to protect the effect on stock price from negative press for *Erika Young's Lifestyle Balance*? And with the ease he'd had even as a teenager, he changed the subject. 'Did Skunk smoke this barbecue? It's great.'

And the conversation went on with discussions on the varied schools of thought on barbecue. Wet sauce or dry rub. Memphis or Texas.

The Friday night barbecue was a casual event. Children could come if you wanted to bring them. Old yearbooks were spread across a table, and everyone wore a nametag with a photo from senior year, from days when the hairstyle mattered more than the percentage of gray – or whether or not you still had any hair. Some people really did still look almost the same. With others, gray hair, less hair, more weight, life had made a difference, and it was only when you saw the smile that you could see the sixteen-year-old who was still in there. Forms asked for updated addresses, phone numbers, family information, email addresses. Groups clustered and separated, circulating and reforming. You'd see some people heading back to the kegs again and again and think, some things never change. Then again, you'd see somebody who had been a serious partier in the old days nursing a Coke and realize some things did. It was catching up time, as if someone had hit the refresh button on the computer and all the information, all the pictures were instantly updated.

As things were breaking up, I heard Fly's voice again. 'So, you're a travel agent now, Campbell? I wish I'd known that.' I turned to find him behind me. 'I travel all the time; we could use a good corporate agent. OK if I call you?'

'Sure, of course.' That was not an account I'd turn down. I still had some pride, but I wasn't stupid about it. I dug in my purse for a card. Office, home, cell phone, address, Twitter, Instagram, website, email address. 'Here.'

'Hillsboro Village. I drive through there every day, and it never occurred to me that I was passing your door.'

I smiled. What was I to say to that? 'Well. Now you know where we are.'

'I'll stop by next week.' He smiled, too. 'I'll take you to lunch.'

THREE

Do you remember . . .
The stars in the sky . . .
Our dreams for tomorrow . . .
A faith in forever . . .
The night's last goodbye . . .
Do you remember?

Stick Anderson

Saturday morning was the grown-up version of the start of a high school dance: boys on one side, girls on the other. The tension was gone, though, replaced with a kind of relief. The men played a golf tournament; the women had lunch at a tearoom and shopped at nearby outlet shops.

'So what did you think?' Barbara asked over Jockey boxers for her sons.

'Think about what?' I asked.

'Fly Young.'

I shrugged. 'He said he needed a travel agent. That would be a good account.'

'I mean about him being single again. And coming to find you.'

'He's not single. And he wasn't looking for me. I've been in the phone book all these years. He was looking for an empty chair.'

'I had very good feelings about this reunion.'

I ignored her and went to pajamas.

That's when my mobile phone rang.

'Hey, this is Fly.'

'Hi.' I'd expected a client, maybe my mom.

'I'm shooting garbage here. I've sliced every ball I've hit. How's the shopping going?'

'Fine. I guess. I'm just along; I'm not seriously shopping.'

'Want to ditch it? Meet me?'

'Ah, no, I don't think so, Fly. Barbara rode with me.'

'Yeah, you're probably right. I guess I ought to stick this out, too. Lucky thing it's a scramble. I don't think we've used one of my shots yet.'

'Well, it's a great day to be outside, though.'

'Yeah, yeah. Are you staying at your parents' house this weekend? How about if I pick you up tonight? It'd give me a chance to say hello to your parents, give us a chance to catch up a little more.'

'I . . . well . . .'

'Come on. You're probably the best friend I ever had. I've missed that.'

I hesitated, but, after all, it would only be a ten- to fifteen-minute ride from my parents' house to the dinner. 'Sure. OK. I'm sure Mom and Dad will be glad to see you.' I wasn't sure of that at all. My mother had never trusted Fly. My dad thought any boy who would choose any other girl than his daughter must be a fool. 'I have to be there a little early to help make sure everything's set up.'

'No problem. You just say what time.'

'Six?'

'Six. I'll see you then.' A click and he was gone.

'Anything up?' Barbara was waiting at the door.

'No. Just . . . I'm going to ride with Fly tonight.'

'I told you. I had a very good feeling about this reunion.'

FOUR

Do you remember?

Stick Anderson

What is it about first love anyway? I heard Fly's voice on the phone, and he sounded just like he did twenty years ago. I might have been seventeen, waiting for his call to tell me when he'd be by to pick me up on a Saturday night, to decide if we were going to Murfreesboro to a movie or just hang out at my house. I don't spend a lot of time thinking about regrets, so I hadn't pined for Fly all these years. But I suddenly realized that I had measured every relationship through my adult life against that teenage passion. Not really comparing the men I met to Fly, but comparing how I felt about them to the way I felt at seventeen in love for the first time. And none of those feelings had ever been quite the same.

I thought it was growing up. I had decided long ago that mature love between two adults wasn't supposed to feel like first love. That maybe that head-over-heels, can't-breathe-right feeling was what was wrong with adolescent infatuation. I thought I wasn't supposed to feel that way anymore. But maybe the truth was I had never really been in love since then.

I have very strict rules about dating married men. I don't. And I assume every man is married until proven otherwise. Separated, I've learned over the years, can mean most anything. It can mean I sign the papers tomorrow or my wife's not in sight right now. It occurred to me to wonder if Fly's wife Erika knew they were separated, but I probably wasn't being fair to him. And none of this really mattered because this wasn't a date; it was a ride.

When Fly pulled into my parents' driveway in a red Corvette, I knew it was going to be a ride down memory lane. He had always wanted a Corvette. It was, all those years ago, his adolescent dream car. I was glad to see he had it, but I had to laugh. What a cliché of mid-life crisis. And, yes, I was watching out the window.

I came into the den just as my mother opened the door. 'Hello, Franklin. It's nice to see you. How is your mother?' Fly's dad had died a few years ago; my parents had gone to the funeral.

Fly was a millionaire, the kind of guy the mayor and governor automatically put on important business and community task forces, but in front of my mother he was a scared teenager. And that was before my father spoke. I half expected to see zits appear. 'She's doing well, Mrs Hale. She asked me to say hello to you both.'

'You tell her hello from us. We talk to her once in a while at the catfish place, but I don't believe we've seen her lately.'

The catfish restaurant was one of my parents' favorite places to eat Sunday dinner after church. It competes with the Cracker Barrel, and, between the two, you can see half the town.

'I'll tell her you asked about her.'

'I guess we'd better go, Fly,' I put in. 'Betty and Pam are expecting me to help with the centerpieces.' I was beginning to feel like a teenager myself.

'Sure.'

I kissed Mom and Dad goodbye and headed out the door.

'Y'all be careful.' Some things did never change, but my mother bit back asking what time I'd be in. I appreciated her effort.

'You handled that well,' I told Fly.

He grinned. 'Your parents always did make me nervous, but it was your brother who scared me to death. If I had to wait for you, he'd just stare at me, never say a word.'

'It was deliberate.'

'But your parents look great. They don't look like they've aged a bit.'

'Yeah, they do whatever they want to do. I feel very lucky.' We'd reached the car. 'You got your Corvette. I'm glad.'

'I always said I'd pull up in your driveway some day in a Corvette and take you away.'

I laughed. 'You did. It's been a while, though. I'd given up expecting it.'

'I never forgot. I meant it,' he said, suddenly serious. 'I meant everything I said to you.'

Right. Something about him made you want to believe even though I could think of several reasons to think otherwise, but I didn't want to go there. I wasn't here for closure. I just wanted to have a good time.

FIVE

I remember when we were eighteen
Everything was out there and waiting
On the top of our world,
   our very small world
We'd found everything that mattered
You and me, when we were eighteen

When we were in school, everybody and his cousin had a garage band, so the music at our dances was always live. For this reunion, though, instead of a band we'd opted for a disc jockey to save money. But the DJ had all our favorite songs. I danced all night – not with Jeb, of course. He and Mailene seemed very happy. I danced with Barbara's husband and Melinda's, probably because Barbara and Melinda told them to ask me, with Ronald, who was always the best dancer in the class. I'd forgotten how much fun it was – and how much fun I'd had with these people, most of them anyway. At our first reunion, ten years after graduation, besides the whole Jeb fiasco, there was a little too much posturing, too much 'look what I've done'. This time around, after twenty years, we were just glad to be there, glad to have survived. We'd lived long enough to go through some tragedy; a few of us hadn't survived. Maybe what had happened was what we'd always hoped for and feared. We'd become grown-ups.

Finally, just for old time's sake, I danced a slow one with Fly. I danced with my head against his shoulder and suddenly recognized the smell of his skin. How long does a memory like that hide? Along about the third verse of 'Whiter Shade of Pale', Fly whispered in my ear. 'What did happen to us, Campbell? How did I ever let you get away?'

It didn't seem to need an answer. What did it matter after all these years? Besides, the honest answer wasn't at all romantic. What happened was that Fly had wanted to be with someone else more than he'd wanted to be with me. At seventeen, that had devastated me, but I had survived worse things since.

'I remember the first time I danced with you,' he said. I tried to think. I remembered dancing with him, but no specific memory stood out. 'At the old fire hall.' The city had let us clean up an old unused fire hall for dances, chaperoned by parents, limited to teenagers. Very Andy Hardy, but it was that kind of town. He went on, whispering in my ear. '"Whiter Shade of Pale". I kissed you and cut my lip on your braces.'

I pulled back and looked at him in surprise. 'Really?' I almost laughed, but he was serious. Smiling, but serious.

'You don't remember?' The smile turned rueful. 'I've never forgotten.'

'I'm sorry.'

'It's OK.'

'I mean about your lip.' I smiled.

Fly shrugged and laughed. 'It was worth the pain.'

We ended the song with an ambiguous hug, and the moment ended, too. We all clapped, circled up for a group photo and hug and sang our alma mater. We promised each other and ourselves that we'd write more often, we'd email, we'd get together more often. And, at the time, we really meant it.

Several of us pitched in, cleared the tables and helped clean up. It was nearly one when the last of us were in the parking lot, hugging one last time, saying goodbye.

'Next week?' Pam asked.

'Next week. Probably Thursday. I'll call you.' We'd made plans to meet for lunch.

Fly and I walked to his car, the summer night air cool and sweet. He put the top down and pulled slowly out of the parking lot.

'It's been great to see you, Campbell. I've thought about you a lot, wondered what you were doing, how you were.'

I didn't know what to say to that. I just rode, listening to Mary Chapin Carpenter on the radio singing about a simple life getting complicated.

'Why is it you've never married?'

I never know how to answer that. Before I came up with anything, he spoke again.

'That's a stupid question. I guess what I really want to know is if you're involved with anybody, if, I don't know, if there's some guy you're going to call tonight . . . tell about what happened, who looked old and who you didn't recognize, about . . .' He took his hand off the gearshift and covered mine, laughed a short, nervous laugh. 'About this old boyfriend you danced with.'

Still not an easy question. 'I don't know exactly. There is a man. We're friends, maybe more. I'm not sure exactly what we are.' I was pretty sure I didn't want to talk about Sam to him.

'Well, I can speak from experience. If he doesn't do everything he can to hold on to you, he'll regret it for the rest of his life.'

This was not at all what I had expected from this night. 'Fly . . .'

'No, I'm not . . . I don't know. Can we just talk a little? I meant it when I said I'd missed you, missed the friend you always were.' Instead of turning toward my parents' house, Fly turned away from town, toward the lake. That's where we used to go on Friday and Saturday nights all those years ago, parking on some old country road that ended at the waterline once the lake bed was flooded by the Corps of Engineers. I decided it was time for a reality check.

'Fly, what happened to us was that you wanted to date somebody else. A new girl moved to town, and she was cuter than me or . . .' Fly started to protest, but I went on. '. . . or more fun than me or sexier than me or just newer than me. I didn't break your heart; you broke mine. But it's OK. That's what happens to kids. I got over it a long time ago. My heart's been broken more than once since then. I mend. I don't think an old girlfriend, even if you really were a fool to let me get away, is the answer for you right now.'

'Now, see? That's what I mean. You always were straight with me.' He pulled into a marina parking lot. Over the years, most of the old roads had been removed. Recreation areas, boat ramps and marinas had replaced them. There were security lights where once there had just been the stars and a moon. He turned off the engine and headlights.

'Are you happy with your life, Campbell?' Fly settled into the corner on his side of the car, facing me. I turned to face him and leaned back against the door on my side.

I thought about it. 'Yeah, Fly. I mean, it's not that I don't have some regrets. I'd do some things differently. And I always thought I'd be married by now, have at least a couple of children. My life is not . . . exactly how I thought it would be, but I'm happy. I like my job, my friends. I like my house. I like my life. My friend MaryNell says that's why I haven't married, that I like things the way they are too much.'

'Is she right?'

'I don't know. I don't think so. Maybe. I know I don't want to change my life . . . just to be married. I've seen too many bad marriages. But I think, I think a good marriage can add . . . a lot. I don't want to change my life unless it's going to be better.'

'What would make it better? If you could wake up tomorrow morning in your dream life, what would it look like?'

I looked at the lake, quiet now and still. 'I guess I'd be married, have those two kids. My husband would talk to me, listen to me, be glad to come home to me in the evenings, glad to wake up next to me. He'd laugh and make me laugh.' I turned back toward Fly. 'He'd be happy, too.'

'Sounds nice.'

'Did I mention the beach house?' I laughed. 'There's a beach house in there somewhere.'

He laughed, too. 'And the guy? The man who's not here tonight? How does he fit into this picture?'

I shrugged. 'I don't know. He's a single father, has a teenage daughter. Right now, she's the most important relationship in his life. Sometimes I think we're very close; sometimes I think we're just pals. I like him. Except when he makes me furious. He's a homicide detective. That's a profession that's tough on relationships.' I shrugged again. 'I don't know.'

'And the clock's ticking?'

'I guess. The clock's always ticking about something.'

'You're right there.'

'What about you? What happened with you and Erika?'

'The truth?'

'What else is worth the time?' I asked.

'It makes me really uncomfortable to admit this.' He stopped. The night air was cooling, reminding me of other nights by this lake, of one in particular. 'I work too much. No question there. I have invested myself in building a business. I've done a good job. I've built a strong company that's financially solid, good employee relations, better benefits than the market. It's a good business, and it's made me a lot of money. My wife and kids enjoy that money; so do my employees and my partners. So, yeah, I've put my life into my work. But, more than that, I don't think I married a wife; I think I chose an accessory. I'm not proud of that; I'm being honest. I think it was pretty much the same for Erika. She had plans of her own, and I fit into them. She looked right, dressed right, drove the right car, made the right friends. We picked the right church, the right neighborhood, the right schools. The money I made gave her a stake for her own start. And it all paid off for all of us.' He stopped again. In the silence that stretched, the chorus of crickets and katydids, summer night sounds in the South, seemed to swell. I waited. 'That's just not enough anymore. For either one of us, I think,' he finished.

I didn't know what to say.

'I guess it's too late to take back that truth thing,' I offered.

Fly laughed. 'Yeah, you asked for that, didn't you?'

Was I supposed to feel sorry for him? He'd made his choices, gotten everything he wanted, and now he wanted it the other way. He wanted one last chance for true love and his stock options, too. But I did feel sorry for him. Sorry, not sympathetic.

'So you just say, "Oops. Changed my mind. Do over?" Does it work that way?'

'Not without a generous settlement.'

'What about your kids?'

He shrugged. 'I don't know. They're so involved in their own lives. You're about to tell me that's a cop out, aren't you? I honestly don't know how they're going to feel about it. I hope they're not as shallow as I'm afraid they are. I guess I need to get to know them. I mean, I've gone to the plays, the ball games, the school deals. I've been there – physically. I can tell you who their best friends are; I know their friends' parents. But I can't say I really know my children as people.'

'Just as accessories?'

'Yeah. I guess so.' He tugged at the knot of his tie, loosening it. 'That's not enough anymore either.' His hair, still sandy, but shorter now than twenty years ago, reflected a gleam from the security lights. He still looked as good as he had back then. Better, really. How unfair is that, that women age, and men, some men anyway, mature, grow distinguished? And how shallow must I be for that to matter? He unbuttoned the top button of his shirt. 'Do you remember the last time we came here?' he asked.

I remembered. It was hot and humid, August in Tennessee, and it was magic. My cotton dress – white with green dots, I think – stuck to me, and my hair, long then, hung straight. We made out, kissed until we couldn't breathe. Passion within the rules. Then we sat on the hood of his parents' car, cooling as the night did, watching the moon shine through the mist rising off the lake. It was magical, other worldly. We talked about the future. Our future. College – and after. Where we'd live. How many children we'd have and when. And the red Corvette, of course. I remembered. I might go back and be a teenager again if it could all be like that night – or like I thought it was that night.

'I love you,' he said that night. 'I'll always love you, Campbell.' And I believed that he would.

I found out later he was already seeing the new girl.

I shivered. From a breeze off the lake or . . . what? A lost dream, a narrow escape?

Fly reached over and took my hand. 'I wish I could go back to that night, that boy, that girl. I . . . I took a wrong turn about then, and I never knew how to turn around and get back on the right track. I know, I know. You're right; you don't get do overs in life. But, like it or not, I'm having to make some changes. I just want to get it right this time.' He lifted my hand to his lips and kissed it softly. 'And I guess I wanted to say I'm sorry. I am, you know. I've been sorry for a long time.'

We looked at each other for what seemed a lifetime, twenty years at least, looking for confirmation, forgiveness, a time machine?

Finally, Fly nodded. 'I'd better get you home.' He laughed. 'I still wouldn't want to have to face your daddy when he's really mad.'

Just like all those other times, he drove me home. We stood on the steps at my parents' back door, and he kissed me good-night. My mother, like all those other times, was awake in her bed but pretending not to be. And, just like all those other times, I went to sleep smelling his skin and his aftershave, still feeling his lips on mine.

SIX

Just an ordinary small town boy
With dreams of a big, wide world
Just an ordinary small town boy
In love with a small town girl

Stick Anderson

I went to church with my parents – and to the catfish place for Sunday dinner – so it was mid-afternoon before I got home. Back in Nashville, I pulled into my shaded drive on the bank of the Cumberland River with relief. I didn't want to be seventeen again. Not on most days, anyway. I took the Sunday *Tennessean* and a glass of iced tea out to a shady spot on the patio at the back of my house. I read the local news, the sports, the comics. Below me, the Cumberland River kept moving, green, muddy water on its way downtown, west then north to spill into the Ohio just above the Tennessee, then down the Mississippi to the Gulf of Mexico. From there, the seven seas. I just sat there on my patio and watched it go. Summer laughter floated up, speedboats passed by, the occasional skier tagging along.

The day was hot, and moisture condensed on my glass. First love. Why was it that for some people first love was like a first car, something to drive just to get around until you got the one you really wanted? And some people married their high school sweethearts and stayed together forever, growing first up, then old together. Had I been a fool, seeing the blond, good-looking quarterback with the easy smile and not noticing that he had no character? Or had I seen something else, something better that was inside him? Would he have been a different person, a better man if we'd stayed together? If I'd had a little less pride, been a little more forgiving back then, would I have the two kids today? And the beach house? Would I be glad or sorry this afternoon?

I was just folding the last of the paper, not remembering a thing I'd read, when the phone rang.

'Campbell?' When I heard my friend MaryNell's voice, I was surprised at how disappointed I was. I realized I'd been hoping Sam would call.

'How was the reunion?' MaryNell asked. 'What did you end up wearing?'

I told her. I told her about the girl from chemistry class who had become a research biologist with NIH, and the guy who was the closest thing our class had had to counter culture. 'All these years I'd imagined him underground somewhere, involved in some subversive group, nonviolent, of course. Nope. Nuclear engineer. Working for the government. Another illusion shot.'

I told her what a pleasant surprise it was to find out people had outgrown the pigeonholes I hadn't realized I had put them in – and what a shock it was to realize that some people thought I should stay in a pigeonhole myself. I told her about Jeb and Mailene. And I told her about Fly.

'He sounds like bad news to me,' she said. 'Like he's looking for an emotional caretaker.'

I shrugged. 'It doesn't matter. If he calls about travel arrangements, great. I can always use the business, but I learned my Fly Young lesson a long time ago.'

'Who'd have thought it? Erika Young with her perfectly balanced life. She's always reminded me of Gwyneth Paltrow, her balanced lifestyle blog. Have you ever tried Erika's diet? Excuse me, her lifestyle?'

'No. Have you?'

'Yeah. It was kind of weird. There's this group, you know, and it's organized kind of like a class or something. You meet once a week and exercise together; you have these tapes. And the whole group is supposed to be a support system, you know?'

'Did you lose weight?'

'Maybe ten pounds. You pay twenty-five dollars or so for her book, then another hundred and fifty dollars to join the group for three months, your own personal set of tapes included at no extra charge. You're paying nearly two hundred dollars for somebody to tell you to eat normal, healthy meals and exercise more. But if you're overweight it's a character flaw. Your life isn't balanced.'

'Kind of a mixed message?'

'Absolutely. I decided it was a rip-off. You're supposed to listen to the tapes while you exercise on your own, like, for motivation, and it's all just vague, feel good, self-help kind of stuff.'

'A lot of people do it.'

'You figure the leader of the group gets something. They usually meet in free places, community centers, schools, churches. There were thirty-five people in my group. That's . . . five thousand, two hundred fifty dollars. Say the leader gets a thousand. I bet it's not that much, but say it's a thousand. Say the cost of the audio tapes is ten dollars. That's probably high, but even so, you've got four thousand, two hundred forty dollars profit from each one of those groups. That would add up. How many Erika Young Lifestyle Balance groups do you think there are in Nashville alone at any one time?'

'No telling.'

'Exactly. And then you've got the maintenance groups and the seminars and the books and the Erika Young Lifestyle daily calendar, your motivational videos and on and on. She's made a ton of money.'

'Yeah, I guess they both have.' We thought about that for a minute or so.

'And what about Sam?' MaryNell asked.

'What about Sam?'

'I'm on Sam's side. He's solid, a good father, and—'

'There is no side!' I interrupted.

'And he can carry a gun so you'll feel safer.'

'That's what I've been waiting for in a man,' I said dryly. I changed the subject. 'I'm thinking about getting a cat. What do you think?'

'I've been telling you for years that you need a cat, but I'll believe it when I see it.'

We talked a little longer, then, just after we'd hung up, the phone rang again. I thought it was MaryNell calling back with more about what was wrong with my love life, and I really was tired of that. I almost didn't answer.

'Campbell?' Sam! I realized how much I wanted to see him, how badly I wanted to talk to him about . . . about everything.

But all I said was: 'Hey.'

'OK if I come by later?'

'Sure. When?'

'I don't know. I keep thinking I'm about to get wound up here, but things keep coming up. I'll pick up supper.'

'Don't bother. I have sandwich stuff here.'

'OK, well, I'll see you when I can.'

Not especially romantic, but I'd be glad to see him. And there was the gun thing.

SEVEN

There's a world in your eyes
Blue and deep as the ocean
Clear and high as the sky
If I could just fly

Stick Anderson

It was nine thirty before Sam made it. I'd given up on supper and had my ham sandwich hours before. While I fixed one for him, he told me what he could about the case that had kept him at work all weekend. 'Random street crime, I guess, although, you know, that doesn't usually end in murder around

here. Wallet on the ground with no cash. Did the guy get
scared and shoot him? Why not just take the money and run?
An accountant. Software company.' Sam shook his head.
'Wrong place, wrong time.' I put his sandwich on a plate,
added some tomato slices. He leaned against the kitchen
counter, tall, tired and wrinkled, shirtsleeves rolled up,
gesturing with the glass of tea in his hand.

I did like my life, and I liked Sam here in my kitchen. I
liked that he cared about a guy who might have been in the
wrong place at the wrong time.

We moved to the den, and he finished his sandwich. 'Trade
you neck rubs?' he asked.

'Sure. Have a seat. You first.' Sam sat on the floor, and I
settled on the couch behind him. I started kneading his
shoulders and neck. 'How's that?'

'Mmmmm.'

'I'll take that as OK?'

'Mmmmm. How was the reunion?'

I shrugged, but I was behind him, so he couldn't see.

'Tell me about it. Any old boyfriends there?'

I went through the highlights I had already told
MaryNell. I left out the deputy sheriff and the moonshine. I
was afraid he might feel compelled to report it to somebody.

'I think I need to see that nametag,' he said. 'See what you
looked like at seventeen. Where is that yearbook?' I dug my
knuckle into a particularly tight knot. 'Oww! OK, OK. Forget
about the nametag. Just put on your cheerleading uniform, then.'

'Pervert! Are you working Vice these days?' No answer. 'I
danced all night.'

'Hhmmm.'

'I looked great.'

'Of course, you did. You always look great,' he agreed. 'Tell
me all about it.'

I told him more, and he nodded and mumbled to show he
was listening. I decided to tell him about Fly.

'I did see an old boyfriend.'

'Hmmm?'

'My first love. Well, if you don't count Tommy Meacham
in second grade. He broke my heart.'

'Tommy Meacham in second grade?' He leaned his head to the right as I concentrated on his left shoulder.

'No! The old boyfriend at the reunion. He came and sat with us Friday night, and then he picked me up Saturday. It wasn't . . . I mean . . . It was strange. I mean, he's married, says he's separated, but, you know. He's married. He wanted to talk, and we stopped at this marina, close to a place we used to park when we were in high school. I guess it's a mid-life crisis, his marriage is bad and he's trying to figure out what direction his life is going. He even has a red Corvette. I mean, how much of a cliché is that? So we talked a while and then he took me home, to Mom and Dad's, I mean, and he kissed me.' I waited to hear what Sam would say. The silence stretched, and I tensed. What was he thinking?

Then I heard a gentle snore. Sam was sound asleep, his head resting against my leg, hadn't heard a thing I'd said. Not the jealous type, I guess. I touched his hair. This was my life. So much passion that, when I did get a date, I put him to sleep. For the first time in years, I remembered how my brother used to say when we were kids and he went to sleep in church it was because he was comfortable with God. I turned the television on low and watched Hugh Grant in the last half of *Notting Hill* before I moved and woke Sam.

EIGHT

Everything was out there and waiting
We'd found everything that mattered

Stick Anderson

Fly didn't call that week. Not that I'd wanted him to. But he had said he would, so I kept half expecting it, waiting for the other shoe to drop. Same old Fly. We were busy at work, so I didn't really need to take a long lunch anyway.

I did meet Pam on Thursday.

'It was a little strange seeing Fly, though, after all these years,' she said. 'I mean, at first I was excited to see him because I'm leading an Erika Young Lifestyle Balance group right now. It's great. But then he said that they're separated, so I didn't say anything about it. I check the website every day, and since I'm here in town, I talk to their headquarters office all the time. I hadn't heard a word there about any problems between them.'

'Really.' I wasn't encouraging this conversation.

'Not a word. Her program's all about balance, you know. That no one part of your life should dominate, that if you get everything in balance, you're not going to be overworked, overstressed, overtired, so you're not going to overeat. Your emotional life and family life have to be in balance, too.'

'Well, this can't help her image, then, can it?'

'No, I can't believe it. I mean, the videos and website are so full of family pictures, how she and Fly are so happy because they're in balance, how he's got this fabulously successful business, but so does she, so their lives are balanced.'

'You're leading a group?'

'Yeah, I've done it four or five times before.'

'Do you mind my asking how much you make as a leader?'

'Not at all. You ought to try it. If I sign you up as a leader, I get a bonus. I get five hundred dollars for each group, plus a ten percent bonus if the group is over fifteen. And there's a little more bonus for every five more. But you don't do it for the money.'

'You don't?'

'No, it's just great, helps you stay in balance. And it's kind of, I don't know, like a mission, to help other women.'

I nodded, but I was thinking, that's a lot of money without rent and with very little labor cost. I promised to let Pam know if I decided to get up a group so she'd get the bonus, but I was thinking, not a chance in a million. If I'm going to get evangelistic about something, it's not going to be Fly Young's wife.

The following Monday Fly's secretary did call.

'Marcella Andrews. Franklin Young asked me to call you. We'd like you to handle our travel arrangements.'

She knew what she was doing, had the company's principal travelers' official names, preferred airlines, frequent flier numbers, cell numbers, credit card numbers, hotel preferences, everything we'd be likely to need. She emailed me the correct spellings. I hung up feeling very pleased with myself – and relieved. Pleased because Fly's company sounded like a very good account and relieved that I didn't have to deal with Fly's crisis of meaning. Five minutes later, one of Fly's associates called to schedule a last-minute trip to Seattle. He needed a car, preferred full size, four door, and a hotel room, king, non-smoking, lower floor. No problem. This was going to be a very good day.

Fly's company, HealthwaRx, was, in fact, a very good client to have. Fly had two partners, Al Evanston and George Madison. Fly had been a computer techie. Madison's background was business planning and marketing. Evanston was a physician. The company had drawn on each of their strengths to develop a cutting-edge software that was dominating the healthcare software field. The three of them and at least a dozen other senior staff traveled every week. They rarely knew where they would be going far enough ahead of time to take advantage of lower, advance purchase fares. And they were successful enough now not to feel they had to worry about that.

A couple of weeks after I'd started handling HealthwaRx's travel, Fly did come by to take me to lunch. No call ahead of time to ask. He just walked in the door Tuesday morning at eleven forty and said, 'Hey, Campbell, I'm here for that lunch you promised.' I hadn't promised anything, and he hadn't asked if I already had plans, but I wasn't about to mention that when his company was doing a very good job of increasing my profit margin.

'Sure. Let me return this one call.' Fly sat beside my desk and fidgeted while I returned a call from a client who was planning a family cruise for late summer.

'Sure,' I assured him. 'They'll love it. There'll be activities for everybody. There's a kids' club divided into three age groups. The great thing is that kids can have a little freedom, but you know they're on the ship and supervised. They can't get lost. It's a good, secure environment.' I listened. 'Sure. We've got the space held on both ships for a week. The main thing to decide on is the itinerary. Do you want Caribbean or Alaska? OK. Great. Thanks.' I looked up. 'Hi.'

'You ready?'

'Yeah.' I pulled my purse from the drawer and spoke to Lee, one of the other agents. 'I'm going on to lunch now. OK?' Lee nodded, his attention on the conversation in his headset. He waved as we walked out the front door.

'You have to ask? I thought you managed the place.'

I nodded. 'I do. Courtesy. We don't have set lunch times. We just try to be considerate.'

Fly nodded. 'Business good?'

'It's a lot better in the last few weeks. Thank you.'

Fly waved away my thanks. 'We needed somebody. You all are making our lives easier.'

The red Corvette was parked beside the curb. How did he do that? Find a curb spot in Hillsboro Village in the middle of the day? He opened the passenger door and held it for me. When he was inside, I continued. 'Well, I appreciate it.'

'No problem.' He headed north toward town on Hillsboro Road, and we were immediately surrounded by the Vanderbilt University campus. 'South Street, OK?'

'Yeah, that sounds great.' South Street, on Nineteenth Avenue near Division, is a beach dive except it's nowhere near any body of water. The food is good, the chef creative, so you can see anybody there, music producers, politicians, businessmen. The crab cakes are my personal favorite. Most of the seating area is open to the street, and it was an unusually nice day for a Nashville summer. The humidity was low, and we found a table by the large open windows.

After Fly and I had ordered and Fly had a beer, I had my iced tea, Fly leaned back in his chair, bumping into country singer Miranda Lambert at the table behind him. 'Excuse me,' he said over his shoulder, scooting his chair forward. He grinned and, for a second, looked just like the seventeen-year-old Fly I remembered. 'Oops. So, things are working out OK for you, handling our travel? Nobody's being unreasonable, demanding only blue M&Ms in the aisle seat in the third row on every flight?'

'No, unless you're hearing some complaints. Everyone's been great. Your secretary, especially. Very organized.'

Fly nodded. 'Marcella. Yeah, she really runs the place, you know.'

'Well, I guess she has to. You guys are on the road all the time.'

Fly tilted his head in acknowledgment. 'It's true. In all fairness to Erika, you can see why this kind of job is so hard on a family. In the beginning, we were working twelve to fifteen-hour days, talking with the doctors, the administrators, nurses. We even interviewed focus groups of patients.' As Fly talked, he grew more and more animated. 'Al and George and I were best friends, feeding off each other, sure we were going to make a difference. We tried to create software that would do what people really wanted, what people felt they needed. Instead of starting the other way around, starting with what software was already providing and just trying to make it a little better. A lot of the people who work there have been part of the company from the beginning. Marcella, for one. She was Al's office manager when he was in medical practice. And we've done a good job, but things change.' He stopped. 'People change.'

I was beginning to understand why Fly was so successful. He was truly excited about what he was doing. Still.

He went on without ever slowing as the waitress set down our salads. 'In the early days, all the time was going into development. I thought, when we get this done, I can have a life. I gave my family so many mental IOUs, I was like that guy in the commercial who's watching his kid's soccer game over the internet, promising them – and myself – that it was worth it and it wouldn't last forever. It wasn't long before the only one I was kidding was me. They learned to expect an emergency, a real emergency, on the night of the play, the day of the championship, whatever.' He shrugged.

'I don't really think it would have made any difference in the long run for Erika and me.' He looked to the side, perhaps uncomfortable with the admission. 'We married each other for the wrong reasons; we got exactly what we bargained for, and, I think' – he looked back to me – 'we realized we both sold ourselves short.' He smiled ruefully. 'I'm just afraid it's too late.'

What was I supposed to say to that? He was too smart for platitudes. 'I think,' I said slowly, 'that, if you want to change direction, you have to start somewhere, sometime. If you think it's too late to change now, then five years from now, you realize you've wasted five years.'

He nodded, looking down at the table, solemn now. Just then, the waitress returned.

'OK. Sorry for the wait, folks. Blue Plate and for you the crab cake basket with squash casserole instead of fries. Everything look OK?' Quick pause. 'OK, your beer OK? I'll get you some more tea. Be right back.' She was gone.

'The thing is,' Fly continued, 'it never stops. Now, we don't put as much time into development, but it's training, implementation, hand-holding. I may not be putting in fifteen-hour days at the office all the time, but I'm still traveling every week.'

He took a bite of squash casserole, then went on. 'You have to be the guy who thinks of it first. Always. You have to be the guy they can call when they want a program that will do the next thing. You have to be the guy they believe can think like them, only sooner, better. If you're not that guy, it doesn't matter who you are. You've just got flat, plastic circles in boxes on shelves. In this business, if you're not first, you're out of the game.'

I could see that it wasn't the kind of job you could just slow down at. They worked intensely and played the same way. Fly told me about the partners' meetings they had had through the years. 'We have to let some steam off somehow, so we try to make a couple of trips a year, get out of the office, totally out of the office, talk strategy and not details.' Skiing in Peru, diving in the Red Sea, sea kayaking along the Alaskan coast. Even their vacations couldn't be mediocre. 'We need to talk to you about the next one. We're thinking about Kilimanjaro.' I could do that. 'We need to get away. Just the three partners. Work through some stuff.'

Fly shrugged. 'There are a lot of things I really like about my job. I don't mean to whine. I like what I do, and I'm good at it, but things change. I like the perks, the trips, the money. I just don't like what happened to the rest of my life.'

'So, what will you do? You said you're going to change your life. How do you do that?'

He shrugged again. 'I don't know.' He smiled a little sadly. 'Sail off into the sunset? Maybe I was hoping you'd help me figure that out. You always seemed to have your head on straight. You always knew who you were.'

'Fly, I can't . . .'

'I know. I know. You don't want to get in the middle of this. Erika and I have got to figure out what we're going to do. I know that has to come first. But your friendship is important to me. I don't want to let that go again.'

There were a few moments of silence as we looked at each other. 'OK,' I said. 'I can be your friend. But, as your friend, the first thing I want to tell you is to take care of your family. You won't have another chance like this with your children. You don't have long with them before they're gone. You said yourself that they're very involved with their own lives now. This is your chance to get into their lives, too.'

'You're right, of course. Easier said than done.'

I nodded. 'Yep. Easy for me to say, too, not having any children. But I see too many people, you do, too, who try to fix what's wrong in their families by starting over. New family. New chance to do it right. Don't do that. Whatever happens with you and Erika, be a father to your kids, these kids, while they still are.'

He nodded. 'Yeah, in fact, that's one thing I want to talk to you about. I want to take Cooper on a trip. Alaska. Do some fishing, kayaking, hiking. Can you set that up for us?'

'Sure, of course. That sounds like a great idea. When do you want to go? How long?'

'Cooper starts football practice at the end of July, need to work around his football schedule, scrimages and the start of the season. Ideally, I'd like it to be in the next few weeks. Is that enough time?'

'This is peak time for Alaska, but I'll check and let you know. Let me know what dates I have to stay away from?'

'I didn't bring my calendar. I'll call you when I get back to the office, but I think I can schedule around it. If a crisis comes up, somebody else will just have to handle it. Because you're right. This may be my last chance with Cooper.'

The rest of lunch was lighter, catching up, and when Fly dropped me off I promised to get the Alaska information together for him that afternoon.

Lee's eyebrows went up as I came in the front door. He could see the Corvette through the glass front of the office. Luckily, he was on the phone, so I didn't have to hear any commentary.

Two hours later, I had a tentative package put together for Fly and his son. I had a fishing guide set up, sea kayaking, several days in the Anchorage area and a few in Denali. It was tough to find space on such short notice during Alaska's busiest time, but it helps when you aren't on a tight budget. I called Fly, went over the details with him, and had the whole thing confirmed before five. I left the office feeling very good about helping Fly and his son connect. It didn't hurt that the commission on the trip would help me connect with a new leather chair I'd been lusting for.

NINE

Do you remember?

Stick Anderson

The next day, the coach of a women's basketball team called. His team was going to the Bahamas to play a tournament. The tournament would include nationally ranked teams, out of the league of this small college team. But the program was a good one, aggressive and determined, and the coach thought playing ranked teams would help his women improve, help them play better in their own conference. Besides the Bahamas would be fun. Planning a trip like that every year helped recruit players to the small West Tennessee town.

The coach was encouraging alumni, parents, fans and other

friends of the program to come along, and we were still working out the details: hotels, air, vans, meals, shows. What sights should they not miss? What excursions might they like? I made notes. Some decisions had been made before I had produced the brochure he had distributed to promote the trip, but we were still refining the itinerary. The deadline for commitment was little more than a week away. The final number would determine some of our decisions, and we wouldn't know that until the last minute, the day after the last minute, more likely, because that's when some people always make up their minds. I told him I'd fax him a couple of sample itineraries the next day, and we both hung up feeling we'd accomplished something.

The next call was from Sam. 'How about dinner this weekend?'

'Sure. What'd you have in mind?'

'I'm thinking the Blue Moon,' he said. 'Let's shoot for Friday. If something comes up, we'll do it Saturday.'

'OK. I love the Blue Moon.'

'I know.'

It was a good day.

TEN

Do you remember . . .
A soft, warm, summer night . . .
My fingers in your hair?

Stick Anderson

It's funny the way you go along never noticing something, and then suddenly it's everywhere. Like an old song you haven't heard for years, then suddenly it's on every radio station you listen to. That's the way it was with Fly and his HealthwaRx company.

Even when I don't have time to read the *Tennessean*, I make a point of going to its website to check out the headlines. And I get the *City Paper* emailed to me every day. On the fourth of July, the local business headline in both papers was about HealthwaRx. The healthcare industry 'giant', and I'm quoting, was about to go public, pending final approval from the Securities Exchange Commission.

'Although the recent murder of HealthwaRx's chief accountant had clouded prospects for the stock issue, interest is high,' one article read. Murdered accountant? Charles Patton. I hadn't heard his name before or where he had worked. Sam's murdered accountant? The IPO price was expected to be twenty dollars per share. The capital generated by the stock issue was earmarked for product development, according to a spokesman for the company. The articles in both papers suggested that the demand for ownership of the 'industry pioneer' would be enormous. Even the *Wall Street Journal* did an article on the stock offering.

Fly Young and his partners stood to make millions if the demand for the new stock was as high as brokers expected. I wondered if I should try to get in on the deal. I pulled out my bank statement. Not enough to spare there. Fly Young hadn't gotten to be a millionaire by letting a little thing like not having money stop him. Fly Young would borrow the money to invest in a sure thing. No guts, no glory. Why was I so afraid to take a chance?

I went home for the Fourth of July, ate my mom's hamburgers and my dad's homemade ice cream, and sat in a lawn chair by the side of the road to watch my nephews riding on a fire engine and waving flags in a small town American Fourth of July parade.

'I heard Fly Young was back for your reunion,' my brother said.

'Yeah.'

'Mom said you went with him.'

I grimaced. 'I rode with him. Not exactly the same thing.'

'I never did trust him.'

'I know,' I said. 'You told me often enough. And he still remembers. He said he's still scared of you.'

My brother laughed. 'Good. Are you seeing him again?'

'He's married!'

My brother raised his eyebrows, his eyes still on the parade, but didn't say anything.

'I am not seeing him. His company is a client now, a good client, and I appreciate that, but it's all business. I had lunch with him day before yesterday. A business lunch.'

My brother nodded. He drank a swig of Coke and looked at me over the can. I started to say more, but I didn't want to protest too much.

I got home in time to watch fireworks from my patio. The stones warmed my bare feet with the day's stored heat. The sky sparkled with fireworks over the river at Riverfront Park downtown. Just to the left, I could see the display from the Sounds game. Behind me, if I cared to stand up, were the fireworks from the water park at the lake. Bright sparkles were lighting up the sky all over the country beyond what I could see. Maybe there had been a few technological advances. Maybe budgets were bigger, but for years and years it had been pretty much the same. Just like when Fly and I would sit wrapped in a quilt to watch smaller fireworks in a smaller town. It didn't feel small. It felt like the whole universe was putting on its best show just for us, just because we were so much and so purely in love. Diamonds, rubies, emeralds and sapphires on midnight blue velvet all over the sky. I went inside to get a sweatshirt as the air cooled and watched till the last light faded, the last muffled pop quieted, the last smoke drifted, and the night was still.

ELEVEN

Friday night Sam was almost on time. When I opened the door, he looked decidedly un-detective-like in khakis and light-blue Oxford cloth.

'It's a beautiful night,' he said. 'Great night to take your Spider. Take the top off, feel the wind in your hair.' He reached out and brushed my hair back behind my ear.

'You can't fool me, Detective. You just want to drive it.'

He nodded, smiling. 'Busted. But it is a beautiful night.'

I couldn't argue. Perfect weather, warm, not too hot, not too humid, honeysuckle in the air. 'You're right. The top's already off.'

My 1960 red Alfa Romeo Spider was my one real luxury. My dad had bought it for me very used when I was in college, and I'd been driving it ever since. Except for several months in the past year when it had been in rehab at AAAAuto. A run-in with a bullying Mercedes and an oak tree on an icy night had nearly totaled both of us. The Spider was older; it took her longer to bounce back. Charlie, the owner of AAAAuto, had searched the internet to find parts and gently nursed her back. Her new paint job was even the same color. Charlie had taken good care of her, but she and I were both glad she was home.

I handed Sam the keys and grabbed an elastic band for my hair. As romantic as it looks in the movies, the wind in my unrestrained hair just leaves it a tangled mess. We left Sam's anonymous unmarked police-issue sedan in my drive and let the Spider take us past the bright lights of Music Valley Drive. That hum, purr, really. She was happy to be on the road with her top down.

Between the wind and the traffic noise, Sam and I didn't do much talking on our way across town. The night was clear, though, and the lights of the Nashville skyline were beautiful. It was nice to have Sam drive and be able to look around. We took I-440 from pretty much the eastern limits of the town to the west and exited at White Bridge Road. Just west of there, Sam took a left, and we went through an unlikely-looking residential neighborhood until a small sign said Blue Moon Café. One more turn, and we began to see small boatyards. We turned into Rock Harbor Marina and parked.

Like my little house, Rock Harbor is on the Cumberland River, but at the city's western edge, so boats anchored here could sail out of the marina and just keep going. Through the locks at Cheatham Dam, all the way to Paducah, then from the Ohio, wherever you want to go. Take the Tennessee to the Tombigbee in Alabama or keep going with the Ohio to the Mississippi. Either way, once you're in the Gulf of Mexico, it's just you and the sea. So the boats at Rock Harbor tend to be bigger than you'll see at a lot of other marinas in the Nashville area. These, whether sailboats, houseboats or big cruisers, tend to be seaworthy, not simple fishing boats. These boats strain at their lines, ready to get out in the blue water where the seas run deep beneath them. Ready to leave these shallow rivers for the oceans they were made for.

We walked down metal and aged wood gangways to the floating deck that was the Blue Moon's dining room. Candles in cheap hurricanes lit the night, and the boats jostled against each other in their slips. The evening breeze brought the river smell with it, organic, full of equal parts life and decay, God's recycling. The hostess led us to a small table by the rail. 'Ethan will be your waiter tonight. He'll be right with you.' She handed us tall menus and left us.

Sam raised an eyebrow. 'This is nice.' I answered the question there. He smiled.

'Hello. I'm Ethan. I'll be your server this evening. Are you all having a good evening?' Ethan was maybe twenty, gangly, confident of being liked. Short, hair, clean-cut.

'Absolutely,' Sam said. 'How about you?'

'Pretty good.' Ethan grinned. 'Now, what can I get you folks to drink?'

Ethan had brought us water and drinks and was on his way back to take our order when a large sailboat motored slowly in to dock just below us. I was ordering crab cakes when I heard, 'Campbell?' I turned to see Fly tying off lines, making the sailboat fast. 'Campbell? Hey!'

'Fly! Hi.'

He tugged one last line tight on a cleat and jumped off. He looked up. 'I'll be right up.'

I turned to Sam and Ethan, my mouth open to explain, but Fly beat me to it.

'I'll just give you another minute,' Ethan said as he retreated, sensing conflict.

'I didn't expect to see you here,' Fly said. 'How are you? And how is it we've lived in this town all these years without running into each other before now?'

'Fly, this is Sam Davis. Sam, Fly, uh, Franklin Young.'
Sam and Fly shook hands.

'Good to meet you,' Fly said. 'You must be the policeman.'

'Fly's a friend of mine from high school,' I explained. I felt somehow that I was way behind and trying to play catch-up in some game I didn't even know the rules to.

Sam nodded, several questions in his eyes.

'Campbell didn't tell you?' Fly asked. 'We hadn't seen each other since graduation until our reunion a couple of weeks ago. Campbell was my first love, you know.'

It might be true, but this wasn't the way I wanted to tell Sam about it. 'Long time ago.' I smiled, feeling suddenly like a referee in a fight. I saw Sam had on his cop face, taking everything in and giving nothing away. He nodded.

'Campbell tells me you're a detective with Metro.'

Sam nodded again. 'That's right.'

'Homicide?'

'That's right.'

Fly's face clouded. 'You, uh, probably know, our accountant was, uh, killed not long ago. About the same time as that reunion, I think. Charlie Patton.'

'Yeah.' Sam wasn't giving anything away.

Fly nodded. 'Terrible thing. Tragic.'

'Yeah.'

'I don't guess you, uh, know anything more? About who did it?'

'Not yet.'

Fly was still standing beside the table. He nodded again. It seemed rude to leave him standing there. I didn't know what to do. Or say.

'Have a seat, Fly,' I said. 'Are you meeting someone?'

'No, and, look, I don't want to intrude,' he said. 'I just stopped by. I'm on my way out of town.'

'On that?' I asked, inclining my head toward the boat.

'Yeah, isn't she great? I just bought her. The *Manana*. I'm sailing her to Florida. There's a boatyard there, does great restoration work.'

'Wow. Did this just come up? I didn't know you sailed.'

He certainly hadn't mentioned anything about it when we'd had lunch. Not that he had to tell me his plans.

Fly sat as he continued talking, obviously excited about the boat and his trip. 'Yeah, I took an off-shore course a couple of years ago. I've chartered some, but this came up, got a great deal, and I couldn't pass it up.' A shadow clouded his face. 'And there's some business I need to check into.' He laughed, but it didn't sound as if he meant it. 'There's always some business. But don't worry. I'll be back in time for the trip with Cooper.'

Ethan came back. 'Ready to order? I don't want to rush you. I'll be glad to come back. Could I get you something to drink, sir?' he asked Fly.

'No, no, I'll just get another table.'

'Join us,' Sam said.

I looked at him. He looked perfectly amiable, but there was something in his voice, a challenge? A spider spinning a hammock for a fly to rest? And who was the prey – Fly or me? The Blue Moon was one of my favorite restaurants, but right then I wished I could be almost anywhere else.

'You're sure?' Fly turned to the waiter. 'I'll have some bottled water, flat. Whatever you've got is fine.'

'Yes, sir.' Ethan left.

'Where were we?' Fly said. 'Homicide, is that right?' Fly seemed ill at ease. Jumpy somehow.

Sam was still, watchful. He nodded.

'Tough job. I admire you. I know this has been horrible for us. To have to deal with it every day . . .' Fly shook his head. 'And I think Campbell said you have a daughter?'

Sam nodded again. This was not the same man who had picked me up less than an hour ago. This man had narrowed eyes and a hard jaw. And he didn't really look like he was having a good time.

'You've just bought the boat?' At least Sam spoke.

'I did. I've always wanted a boat big enough I could live aboard for a couple of weeks at a time but not so big I couldn't handle her alone. I'll get her refitted, update the electronics, make sure she's seaworthy.' He shook his head. 'When you're sailing, you're going along, skimming the water, riding it. Then, when the wind's just right, it catches the sails, and it's in control.' He looked a little sheepish. 'You're riding the air then. It's like you can fly.'

Sam nodded.

I have never enjoyed the pan-seared trout at the Blue Moon less. Fly talked about his plans, about high school teachers and friends, dances and ball games long past, about the two of us and young love. He laughed, reached over to take my hand when he remembered something funny, something sad. Sam sat back and watched and listened, nodding, prompting Fly occasionally. Anybody watching would have thought Fly and I were lovers, Sam a casual friend. But Ethan had been there from the beginning of the evening. Ethan knew better, and I saw him watching, wondering how this would affect his tip.

Finally, it was over. Fly insisted on paying for our dinner, and he was a generous tipper. Ethan was smiling – and probably better off.

'I'll call you, Campbell,' Fly said. 'I've got my laptop and phone. Can't leave civilization totally behind. But we're all set for Alaska, aren't we?' he asked.

'Yes, that's all taken care of,' I told him. 'When the documents come in, I'll get them to your secretary, if that's OK.'

'Perfect. Sam, good to meet you. Thanks for letting me barge in on dinner.' Fly went inside to confirm his arrangements to spend the night tied up at the marina before starting for the Gulf the next morning.

The boat bobbed gently, bumpers nudging the dock.

TWELVE

L ong ride home.

'The old boyfriend from your reunion was Franklin Young? The Third?'

'Umhmm.'

Then there were several miles of silence.

'You might have mentioned it.' His voice was tight.

'Well, I was trying to tell you about it, but you fell asleep.'

He nodded, muscles moving in his jaw.

'And I didn't know the murder you were investigating that weekend had anything to do with him, not until I read an article about his IPO. You didn't say who it was or where he worked.'

More silence. I tried to make conversation, something I'd never had to do with Sam before. I asked about Julie, what she was doing, the latest installment in her dating life. Would she and her high school boyfriend make the transition to college? Did she want them to? Did Sam want them to? Sam answered questions, but he didn't seem too interested.

When we got to my house, he walked me to the door and handed me my keys.

'Do you want to come in?' I asked, surprised that I felt I had to ask.

'It's late,' he said. 'I'd better get on home.'

I nodded.

We both knew his leaving now had nothing to do with the time. I didn't know what to say. I couldn't thank him for dinner because Fly had paid for it. I couldn't tell him I'd enjoyed the evening. We'd both know that was a lie. I felt like I needed to apologize, but I didn't know what for.

'Well. Goodnight,' I said.

He nodded. 'Goodnight.'

I went inside. He waited on the porch until I had closed and locked the door behind me, and I watched out the sidelight as he walked to his own car and drove off.

I went to bed, early for a Friday night, and tried to read, but I ended up throwing the book across the room as if it were to blame and glaring at Stephen Colbert until he gave up and signed off.

THIRTEEN

I cried when I heard that Fly Young had been lost at sea. Little more than a week before he had been sitting in the chair beside my desk laughing about sailing into the sunset.

I was sitting at my desk, trying not to cry any more, trying to make myself work after Fly's secretary had called.

'He's lost at sea,' Marcella said. 'That's all we know, but it doesn't look good. First Charlie, now this. We're in pieces over here.'

I urged her to let me know if there was anything I could do.

Marcella thanked me. 'I'll call you if we hear anything new.'

He had sailed his boat down the Tombigbee Waterway the morning after Sam and I had seen him, the last time I had seen Sam, too, incidentally. He had sailed out into the Gulf of Mexico and across to Cedar Key, a nod to Travis McGee. After a couple of nights and some minor repairs there, he had bought fuel and some supplies and sailed south, through the Keys to the Atlantic.

Fly had been in contact with his office and his family regularly by phone and email. There had been no sign of any trouble until a storm had come up off the coast of south-eastern Florida.

He had even called me the Friday before. 'I'm flying back the middle of the week,' Fly had said, 'and I need to be in Seattle for a nine a.m. meeting on the Monday after that. Get me a car; mid-size is fine. Book me at the Hyatt for two nights, then back to Nashville on Wednesday after one. OK?'

'No problem. If I have a question, should I just leave a message with Marcella?'

'Yeah, and call her anyway, just to confirm that it's all set up. Marcella's putting all my messages on my voicemail, so I can access them anytime, whenever I get a chance to call in. I tell you what. Email it all to me and copy Marcella, too. That should cover everything.'

'OK. So how's the sailing?'

'It's great, Campbell. I'm loving it. I've chartered a boat from the guy who's going to refit mine. I'm going to spend a couple of days out in the blue water, then fly back. I'm telling you, the minute the kids are out of college, I think I'm going to become Cap'n Fly. You can be my booking agent. Start collecting information on charter boat companies.'

'OK.' Right. I'd give it eighteen months before he was

franchising the operation. Cap'n Fly's charters in every coastal town with a commercial airport. He'd have done his market research. Nothing left to chance.

'No, I'm serious. I probably need to go where there aren't too many already. I'll do some research on it when I get home. I've got plenty of time.'

'Sounds like a plan. Well, have a good time. I'll set this up and get the confirmation to Marcella and you.'

'Great. Thanks. I'll talk to you next week.'

'OK. Good luck.'

'Campbell.'

'Yes?'

'I've had a lot of time to think out here. I really want to talk to you next week.'

'Sure.' I didn't know what he meant, and I wasn't sure I wanted to know, but I could tell from his voice that it was serious.

Not long after that, according to Marcella, he'd bought two six-packs of Samuel Adams, some bottled water, bread, sandwich meat and four apples at the Miami marina where he was docked, boarded the *Floridays*, and sailed out of the harbor for a two-day charter.

The *Floridays* was nearly new, sleek and trim with all the new electronic gear, practically sailed herself, the owner, Captain Dave, had told Marcella. She had the latest GPS satellite navigation technology on board, a life raft with GPS transmitter, shelter tarps and emergency food and water. Fly had the satellite phone he had called me on.

Fly had sailed out of the harbor and, unfortunately, into the path of a summer storm. Marcella said he'd been talking from the boat on Monday afternoon to Captain Dave at the boatyard where he had made arrangements for the refitting, telling them about the storm. Apparently there had already been some damage to the boat, and Fly was asking for instructions and advice. Then the phone went dead. They couldn't raise him again. The Coast Guard had sent out a helicopter and spotted a boat in the general area of Fly's last known contact, but there was no sign of Fly.

FOURTEEN

I was trying to get back to work, to concentrate on plane reservations for a client going to Dallas, simple enough, but I couldn't seem to focus. Then Sam called.

'Are you OK?' There was alarm in his voice, responding to what he heard in mine. 'Campbell?'

'Yes, I'm fine.' I sniffed, making unpleasant, mucusy sounds. 'I'm fine, really. It's a friend, a client, Fly Young. You know, you met him. He's lost at sea.' I reached for another tissue and got myself moderately under control.

'Lost at sea?'

'Yeah, there was a storm. They don't know what happened.'

'Where was he?'

I told him, told him about all the sophisticated electronics.

'Not the boat we saw, then?' he asked.

I guess Sam couldn't help thinking like a police officer. 'No. It was a boat he leased there.' I told him about Fly's trip and his plans.

'You hear of a lot of piracy these days, drug runners, mostly, but it's usually the boats they want.'

'His secretary's going to call me when they hear any more.'

There was silence.

'Look, Campbell, this may be bad timing, but I called to see if you wanted to do something, maybe . . . see a movie tonight. I mean, I understand if you don't . . . I just . . .'

I sniffed. 'Sure.' I hadn't seen or talked to him since the disaster at the Blue Moon. He hadn't called, and it's not that I didn't think I could call him. I am evolved. On a good day. I just didn't know what to say, then a few days passed and a few more. Anyway, I was glad he had called, and I sure didn't want to sit around by myself tonight. I'd prefer Sam's company to my own. And a movie would give us something to do besides talk about the last time we were together, a way to avoid the 'relationship talk'. 'Did you have something in mind?'

'I don't know.' He named the new Denzel Washington movie and the new Kate Winslet, neither of which I had seen. 'No police movies.'

Police movies, Sam said, were either stupid, nothing at all like the reality of police investigation, or too much like work. Sometimes both. He found himself wanting to pull out his notebook, start making notes and delegating assignments, get this thing solved.

'Either one,' I told him. It wouldn't matter. I doubted if I could follow a plot anyway.

'I'll come by about a quarter to seven, OK?'

'Sure. Thanks.'

'And if I hear anything here about Young, I'll let you know.'

I had met Sam when I had found myself mixed up in a murder he was investigating. I was on the scene of what turned out to be a murder, and it was touch and go for a while whether he would ask me out or lock me up. We had eventually become friends, though, and, while the only relationship he was committed to right now was parenting his daughter, we saw each other fairly often. It had evolved into a mostly comfortable, low-key, low-stress relationship that was low-maintenance, too. He wasn't seeing anyone else, and neither was I. But we hadn't made any commitments to each other, either. That was part of what had made that night at the Blue Moon so awkward. We haven't defined our relationship, so we didn't know where the boundaries were. There might be expectations, assumptions on both sides, but we hadn't acknowledged them, not officially anyway.

I switched from the airline reservation system to the internet, thinking I'd check my email so I could pretend to myself that I was doing something. I had mail. I scrolled down, past junk mail, past some confirmations, until I saw the one from Fly. Sender: FLY3@HealthwaRx.com. My hand shook as I clicked on it. I had to do it twice.

'Campbell, Having a good Monday? I am. Except for this little storm. Wish you were here. Is there a chance of that someday? Is it too much to ask you to wait for me? Don't give up on me. See you. Fly.'

My phone rang, but I didn't answer it. I couldn't. I couldn't

speak. I could barely breathe. I looked at the information on
the email again. He had sent it less than an hour before his
last contact with the boatyard. My hand still shook as I hit
the print command. I copied it, too, saved it to a file on my
hard drive. I sat there holding the copy I had printed out for
a long time.

By the time I left work to head across I-440 for home, I
hadn't learned much more about Fly. 'No news,' Marcella had
said. 'I'll let you know.'

FIFTEEN

I like working in Hillsboro Village. It's a little community
within the city, a little like I imagine some of New York's
neighborhoods to be. People know each other by sight, if
not by name. The waitress at Pancake Pantry always seems
glad to see me and remembers how I like my coffee. And the
business people look out for each other. Still, I always feel a
little better at the end of the day when my Spider turns east
on 440 to head back to my side of town. Like a mule smelling
the barn, my dad would say.

I take the Briley Parkway North exit, pass Opry Mills
and the Grand Ole Opry, and turn back toward the river. Just
before the road dead-ends at the river, my little road – No
Tourist Attractions Beyond This Point – slips off to the right,
parallel to the Cumberland River.

The two rivers, the Stones and the Cumberland, used to meet
in Donelson, still do, I guess, at the water treatment plant,
although the progress of Stones River is somewhat impeded by
J. Percy Priest Dam, named for a one-time Tennessee congressman
who had become Secretary of Transportation.

It makes for a lot of winding, can't-get-there-from-here
roads, but there's also a lot of beautiful and fertile river bottom
land around here. Once it was a land of huge farms and plan-
tations: Andrew Jackson's Hermitage, his niece's Tulip Grove
across the road. Closer to the rivers, though, were Clover

Bottom and Two Rivers. Clover Bottom is state property now, housing offices of the state historical commission. There's a mental health facility on the grounds that most people think of now when they hear the name. And the Tennessee School for the Blind is there.

Two Rivers Mansion, on McGavock Pike and once home to the family of that name, is a Metro park now, and some claim it's haunted. You can rent it for parties and weddings, a grand, ambitious Italianate home with ruby glass framing the doors that once welcomed the South's powerful to this land between the rivers.

Now that fertile bottomland holds campgrounds, a golf course, shopping center parking, children's soccer fields. No structure too permanent because once every few decades or so, the rivers reassert themselves, reclaiming their land with floods that will not be controlled. Managed, minimized maybe, but never eliminated. The last one put Opry Mills out of business for a while until it could be rebuilt.

My little house, though, is not in danger. Not from the floods, anyway. I'm perched on a limestone bluff, high above the Cumberland, in a little stone house built half a century ago from the same gray limestone. It's on a quiet street, hidden behind shopping, parking, souvenir shops and vacation condos. Like the faithful remnant of a decimated army, it clings with a few companions to a last bit of land between neon commercialism and the river that brought Nashville's first settlers. Sometimes, when the wind is high or the developers' interest rates low, I feel our hold is shaky.

A canopy of trees closed over me to block the early-summer afternoon sun as I turned onto my road, and I felt home already.

As I went inside, I reminded myself to water the impatiens in clay pots by the front door. The shade around my house is too deep for much of anything else. Hostas, ferns, some periwinkle, mosses, lichens. Showy coral impatiens for color. Some days I feel in danger of being overgrown by primitive plant forms myself.

I made some iced tea, kicked off my shoes, and took the tea out to my patio. Down below, I watched the river current headed for town. This was my favorite spot for thinking or brooding or reading. It was pretty much my favorite spot.

With all the electronic equipment Fly had on board, why would he have headed straight into a storm path? Was he trying to prove something? To himself or the rest of the world? Had the storm come up suddenly or changed course? Surely he would have had on a life jacket. You hear tales all the time of somebody surviving for days at sea in a life jacket. If he'd managed to launch the life raft, he'd be set, but didn't the lifeboat have some sort of location device?. We'll probably find him in Cuba, I told myself, resting up in one of the luxury hotels off-limits to native Cubans, making deals. We'll hear from American Express that his card's been used to pay for spa charges, an expensive dinner for eight. He'll show up on CNN smoking cigars and come home full of plans to partner in a luxury resort as soon as American tourism to Cuba is normalized again. He'll be surprised and sorry that we've been worried. *We?*

I'd been keeping Fly at arm's length. He was married, after all, and I'd heard way too many stories of wives who didn't understand, wives who'd grown in other directions, who didn't care anymore. He sounded like a man who'd gone through a door, though, in that phone call. What had he meant? What did he want to talk to me about? At the time, I hadn't really wanted to know, hadn't wanted to have to deal with it. But now I wanted nothing more than for Fly to be safe and able to tell me exactly what he had on his mind.

I shook my head, decided I was not going to assume the worst, and went inside. When he gets back, I told myself, I'll ask him.

SIXTEEN

The movie I saw with Sam that night might have been good. I'll have to rent it when it comes out on DVD or a streaming service someday and watch it. That night, though, I couldn't focus on it. I was restless. Twice Sam asked me if I was OK, if I wanted to leave. Both times I shook my head, tried to behave, tried to get into the movie.

When we walked out, the hot summer night hit us.

'You're upset about Franklin Young.' It was a statement more than a question.

'Yeah.' There was uncertainty in my answer. 'I'll probably hear tomorrow that he's fine, sittin' in a bar on some island, but, I don't know . . .' I paused. 'I don't know.'

Sam nodded.

I went on. 'Sam, I don't want you to think, I mean, that night at the Blue Moon, Fly made it sound like we were . . . I mean . . .'

Sam was shaking his head. 'You don't have to explain anything to me.'

I could tell he wasn't saying that lightly, and I wasn't sure I liked it. Did I not have to explain to him because I didn't matter to him? Because we didn't have a future anyway? Or that much of a present? Or because he trusted me?

'I just want you to understand,' I said.

Sam was still, waiting, watching, the cop face in place.

I went on. 'I wanted to tell you about Fly. I wanted to talk to you about seeing him, about what happened, which wasn't much. But you fell asleep that night, and I would have, but later it wasn't such a big deal. I didn't want it to seem like there was more to it than there really was.'

Sam nodded, then squinted into the distance. He opened his mouth as if to say something, then stopped and nodded again.

'Have you had any breaks in the accountant's murder?'

Sam shook his head. 'No witnesses. No prints on the wallet, which is a little unusual for a random robbery. But the perp could have just wiped it against his pants.' He shrugged. 'Usually we hear something on the street eventually. Nothing yet.'

Back at my house, Sam came in. I fixed tea with plenty of ice, and we went out to the patio. In the dark, the river was almost invisible. Light would occasionally glint off the surface, make its way through the shadows to us. We weren't talking much, just listening to the river's whispers.

'Odds are, he's fine,' Sam said suddenly. 'You hang around me much, you think people are always dying, but that's because I work in homicide. Only the dead ones get as far as me. Most of the emergencies, most of the missing persons, most of the near tragedies are just that – near.' He reached across the space and took my hand. 'Most times it turns out OK.'

'Thanks.'

We sat like that for a while; then I started to tell Sam about Fly. I told him about high school, about being such a cliché, a cheerleader in love with the football player, about being a teenaged girl thinking she's in love for the first time, how perfect the dream seemed until I woke up from it. Sam listened, laughed, but only at the right places. I wanted him to understand how important Fly had been in my life. Had been.

When I finished, we sat in silence. Then Sam spoke. 'I really wish you hadn't told me this.'

I turned to him, a little shocked and hurt. I had just bared my soul, told him about being in love for the first time, having my heart broken for the first time, and he . . .

'I've got a daughter at home, you know, and I'd really rather not know about this until she's been married ten or twelve years, has a couple of kids . . . I could maybe handle it then without wanting to shoot every boy who shows up at the front door.'

Then I laughed. I couldn't help laughing at the image of Sam answering the door with his hand ready to draw on some poor kid. And kept laughing until I cried and Sam pulled me from my chair to sit on his lap while he held me and stroked my hair.

SEVENTEEN

B y the next day the storm was over in the Caribbean. Calm seas, if a little murky from being tossed in a cosmic blender, the air fresher and clearer than ever. The clean-up started. Search parties were sent out. Fly's partners told the locals to spare no expense. They wanted Franklin Young found, rescued.

I canceled the Seattle reservations and called Captain Dave at the boatyard. 'You know everything we know,' he said. 'The Coast Guard's searching the last known location.'

Captain Dave, operating a boatyard and charter service out of Miami, was not a native Floridian. He didn't sound like he was from the South at all, except maybe south Boston. He'd gone south to live the Margaritaville dream, chartering his boat to make the payments, translating a natural gift for fixing things into restoring boats. He was insured, of course, but when did insurance cover the cost of everything?

He was worried about Fly, but he was almost as worried about his boat. 'It was a heck of a storm, but she's a good boat. And your man seemed to know what he was doing. It's early yet.' I couldn't tell if he was trying to reassure me or himself.

The boat was found later that day and towed in to the shipyard. There was blood on the boom hardware, Coast Guard investigators said, maybe a little tissue. Not much, but, of course, that boat had been in a heck of a storm. It would take time to verify that the blood and tissue were Fly's.

Thanks to the high-tech gear, searchers had a precise location for his last contact, and they went there. Nothing, just blue-green water. Planes flew low, marking grids in the sky and criss-crossing them. Boats did the same thing in the water.

On the second day, a life jacket was found floating. They knew it was from the boat Fly was on; 'Floridays, Miami' was stenciled on it. The jacket had been torn, they said, ripped off. There were some stains, maybe blood. They'd know more soon.

I talked to Fly's wife Erika. It was the first time I had spoken to her. 'He's always done these crazy things,' she said, sounding more annoyed than worried. 'All those guys have. I always told him, "You want to risk your life, just make sure the insurance premiums are paid." Now there's no telling how long it will be before we can get an official declaration of death. I don't know what to do, what to say to the kids.'

I kept a weather map of the south Florida coast on my computer monitor, zoomed in as close as it would go, watching clouds drift across the area where rescuers were still searching for Fly – or debris.

The partners seemed genuinely shaken. It could have been any of them. They had all done outrageously dangerous things with absolute confidence in their invulnerability. Fly would either turn up with an alpha male story to top them all – or they would have to face their own mortality.

EIGHTEEN

When I got home that evening, there was a message from MaryNell. 'Campbell. Hey. Call me when you get home.'

I called.

'You gonna be there for a while?'

'Yeah, sure. I just got home.'

'OK. I've got something for you. I'll be right over.' She hung up.

Fifteen minutes later, MaryNell was getting out of her car with something small sheltered in the curve of her arm.

'OK,' she said. 'It's time.'

She opened her hand and showed me a tiny black-and-white kitten.

'MaryNell . . .' I started to protest.

'You told me you thought you needed a cat.' She cut me off. 'This little guy needs a home. How could you turn him away?'

I shook my head and backed away.

'Really. My neighbor's cat had kittens. She's found homes for most of them, but look at this sweetie.' Just then he opened his blue eyes and mewed at me.

'Ohhh. Why'd he do that?' I asked.

'He needs you.'

'You keep him.'

'My house is already a zoo.' She was right. 'If I bring home one more stray, Roger is going to freak out. Two dogs, three cats. Eighteen fish. Last count. The turtle ran away, and I don't blame him.'

'But I don't need a pet. I'm not home enough.'

'Sure you are. You'll love him. I tell you what, keep him

for a week. If you're not in love, I'll find another home for him.'

I grimaced, but she had me. 'What do I do?'

'I knew you couldn't turn him away. I even brought food.' MaryNell handed the kitten to me and turned back to her car for supplies. She'd brought a self-cleaning litter box (I'd believe that when I saw it), bed, food, litter, toys, even a food-and-water dish. 'Just add water,' she said as she dumped them all in my kitchen.

'Whatever happened to "people should be prepared to have pets"?'

'Your problem isn't lack of preparation; it's fear of commitment.'

'I'm not afraid to commit to a pet; I just don't *want* to commit to one.'

'Just give him a chance. What are you going to name him?'

'I have to name him?'

'Of course, you have to name him. What do you think?'

'Burden?'

'Burden. It's a good thing you're not a parent. Haven't you heard about self-esteem and self-fulfilling prophecies?'

'Oh, please. Psychobabble is bad enough about humans. But cats?'

'If you expect a problem pet, you'll have a problem pet.'

'I don't want a pet.'

'Sure, you do. You, of all people, need a pet, something to nurture, talk to.'

'I am not going to be one of those people who talk to animals.'

'You talk to yourself.'

'That's different. I'm human. I can talk back.'

'People who talk to pets are happier.'

'Where'd you learn that? Facebook?'

'Maybe. A week. You don't want him a week from now, I'll take him back, find someone else.'

I hesitated and was lost.

'Great,' she said. 'And don't make that face. What about Checkerboard?'

'Checkerboard?'

'His name. Because he's black and white.'

'I don't think so.'

'Houndstooth? Bear? Like Bear Bryant's hat? OK, OK. You'll come up with something.'

She was out the door and gone, leaving me holding whatshisname. Ebony and Ivory. No. Too long. Martin's Dream. Nope, too self-important.

I put whatshisname down beside his dish and filled the water and food compartments.

'OK, guy, you're on your own.' I started to leave the kitchen, then turned back. 'And don't think this means I'm going to start talking to you.'

NINETEEN

I went online to look up information on how to housetrain cats. Apparently, the conventional wisdom is that cats train themselves. That was another thing I'd believe when I saw. Then I looked up baby names. I figured I could get some ideas for cat names, too. Justin, Jason, Matt, Andrew. Somehow they didn't seem right. He wandered into my room, exploring and started rubbing up against my ankle. It was annoying, but soft. 'Lion? Simba?' Who are you trying to kid? he asked. At least he looked like he was asking that.

I sat at the computer and stared without seeing anything. Which way would the current take anything floating from the place where Fly was last seen? Had he been knocked overboard? Would he have been conscious or not? The boat survived; what else went overboard with him? What about the life raft? What direction would it go? I looked at my watch. Too late to call Captain Dave. It was an hour later in Miami. First thing in the morning, I promised myself.

I carried the cat, whatshisname, back to his bed in the kitchen four times before I gave up. I thought I wouldn't be able to sleep, but his purring was a soft, white noise, and I slept dreaming that I was dining by candlelight with fine china, crystal and silver on the deck of a boat, unfazed by a storm that forced the boat to keel dangerously from side to side. Waves washed over the deck, but I managed to keep my sandals from getting wet. Gear was sliding around the deck, but the table setting was undisturbed. The table was set for two. I was waiting for Fly to join me. I couldn't see him, but I was sure he would be there. I just waited.

TWENTY

The next morning I had to be up early. I had booked a Walt Disney World package for clients, an extended family with three rooms. They wanted to have breakfast in Cinderella's Castle, and their package included a breakfast with Disney characters. The specific meal, though, couldn't be booked more than sixty days out. Today was sixty days out. The Disney office opened at seven a.m., Eastern time, and by ten minutes before six, Nashville time, I was sitting by my phone, dates, names and reservation numbers in hand. I watched the early weather, counting down the time until I could call. At thirty seconds before six, I started dialing. Too quick. I got the recording, 'Our regular office hours are . . .' As fast as I could, I hung up and hit redial. Still a couple of seconds before six. Ahhh. In, but on hold. And I was on hold for the next twenty-five minutes. By the time I talked to a live person, Cinderella's Castle was fully booked for all seatings of breakfast that day. I could try again tomorrow for the next day. I would, but how did anybody get through? I'd have to be not just up but alert and ready again tomorrow by five forty-five. I groaned out loud, and Zebra – no – mewed in sympathy.

I found a large box to keep Tiger (I was trying to go for a positive self-image, but it wasn't working) from wandering all over the house while I was at work. I put in a towel, his dish, the litter box. 'I'll be back. Don't look at me like that. Think of a name for yourself while I'm gone.' He was mewing plaintively when I closed the door.

I put the Spider's top down before I pulled out of the driveway. It was a glorious day. I planned the day as I drove. First, the Cinderella breakfast, of course. Then, unless there was a crisis at work, I'd call Captain Dave. Next I would try Fly's secretary Marcella. And I thought I'd call my friend Mark and ask him to meet me for lunch. Mark always knew things no one else knew. And no one knew how. Mark was a researcher for the *Tennessean*, and he never divulged his sources.

Traffic even moved smoothly on I-440. I pulled into my parking place behind the building on Twenty-first that housed our office twenty minutes early. Time enough for a cup of coffee from The Pancake Pantry.

I nodded in response to Vince Gill as I stood in line.

'You want a table?' Edna asked. The twenty-year veteran waitress recognized me as a regular.

'Not today, thanks. Just some coffee to go.'

'Cream, right? No sugar.'

'Right.'

'One minute.'

She showed Vince to a booth and scurried to get my coffee. I waived to a songwriter I knew, Gordon Kennedy. Then I recognized who was across the table from him – Paul McCartney! I barely restrained myself from going over and gushing. Edna returned just in time. 'You have a good day,' she smiled as she snapped on the plastic lid.

'Thanks. You, too.'

We had a coffee maker in the office, of course, but the coffee at Pancake Pantry was better, not to mention the rows of racks on the sidewalk with the best selection of newspapers in town. If Mark could meet me early, I might just have to come back for an omelet. I reached for the office door more cheerful than I'd felt since I'd heard the news about Fly. Then I opened it to find an office full of crises.

It was two hours later before every fire was put out and I had a chance to call Captain Dave. The canceled flights were rebooked; the lost hotel vouchers were replaced; the lost passport . . . well, at least the client had the address and phone number of the US embassy and a copy of her passport. She'd have to take it from there.

I closed the door to my office and punched in Captain Dave's number. It was my day for recordings. Captain Dave was gone fishing but would call me back as soon as he returned. Ahoy, yourself.

I called Mark. It was too late to think about brunch at Pancake Pantry.

'How about lunch?' Mark asked.

'Sure. What time?'

'One, one thirty? Let the worst of the lunch rush clear out?'

'Sounds good. Thanks.'

'Don't thank me. You're buying lunch.'

I walked down the street and waited in line to get a table. I watched the every day parade of Hillsboro Village while I waited for Mark. Music industry types mixed with Vanderbilt students, med center staff and businesspeople in the Village. Twenty-first Avenue South runs through the Village, and a few blocks south the street becomes Hillsboro Road. If you followed Hillsboro Road south for thirty miles or so, you'd find the actual village of Hillsboro for which the road was named. Confusing? That's nothing compared to trying to find something on Old Hickory Boulevard in Nashville.

Mark found me frowning at the traffic inching through the Village, even more crowded at lunchtime than usual.

'What's up? When you call out of the blue like that, you usually want something.'

'Do I? I'm sorry. But, yeah, I do want something. What do you know about Franklin Young?'

'Besides that he's missing? What's your connection with Franklin Young?'

I told him. I told him about high school and the reunion and the dinner at Blue Moon. I decided not to tell him yet about the email.

'You mean you could have been Mrs Franklin Young, the third? You could have been a multi-millionaire?'

'Well, no. That's kind of the point. He broke my heart, and I didn't hear from him for twenty years.'

'Franklin Young! I mean, that would have been a whole different life. You'd be a whole different person!'

I looked at him. 'What makes you think that? What makes you think I wouldn't be the same person I am?'

'You know what Everett Dirksen said. "A million here, a million there, and pretty soon you're talking about real money." Real money, forty, fifty million or so, has a way of changing a person.'

'Fifty million?'

'That's cash in the bank, they say, well, just the spending money, not counting the house in Belle Meade, the condo in south Florida, although that technically belongs to the corporation, the house in Aspen, the portfolio, the HealthwaRx shares. There was a house in the Bahamas, Eleuthera, maybe, but they sold it last year. Word was, they were looking for something on Maui. And that's not counting her money, either, the assets of Erika's Lifestyle Balance, Inc.'

'So that sailboat would have been pocket change.'

'Pretty much.'

'So what have you heard in the last couple of days?'

'Only what I read in the paper. I haven't heard any whispers. Of course, nobody at the paper knew about you.'

'There's nothing to know about me.'

'Lakeside tryst? Mrs Young's fortune at risk to a second wife? That could be a motive for something.'

'It wasn't a tryst; it was a talk. And what happened to him was a storm.'

'Well, OK, if you're going to insist on facts.'

I glared at him as the waitress approached, a discrete silver stud piercing her left nostril. 'You guys ready to order?'

'Yeah,' Mark said. 'She's paying, so I'll have an omelet with ham, cheese, onions and jalapenos, maybe some cheese grits on the side.'

I went with the Club Salad.

'Did he at least get you in on the IPO?'

'No, I saw something about it, but I didn't have anything spare to invest. I know those IPOs are usually tied up with big investors. I didn't even try.'

'Worried about insider trading violations?' Mark worked at keeping the bland look on his face.

I considered throwing the bread at him, but it was too good.

'It might be just as well, though,' he went on. 'One guy in Business did say he'd heard a whisper or two that the stock might not perform the way everybody's been expecting it to. There's some talk that maybe the company's a little more cash poor than anybody knew. Enron and Worldspan bookkeeping, maybe. But, after all, the reason most companies go public is to raise cash for one reason or another.'

'You'll let me know what you hear, won't you?'

'Sure. If you'll buy me a blintz for dessert.'

'So much for ethics in journalism.'

He smiled, cheerful and not at all offended. 'You've always told me that's an oxymoron anyway.'

TWENTY-ONE

I talked to Marcella that afternoon. No news, and no news was beginning to be bad news. 'The Coast Guard hasn't said how long they'll keep up the search. There are volunteers out looking, and there's a lot of shipping in that area, commercial and private. Everybody's trying to stay optimistic. He's in shape; he's smart. He's taken the survival courses. If anybody can make it through this, Franklin can.'

Yeah. And in Nashville there was nothing to do but wait.

Wait and plan that college basketball trip to Freeport. So that's how I spent the afternoon. I had to find space in a hotel that had no gaming, no gambling at all. It's an NCAA regulation. NCAA teams have to stay in non-gaming properties even in the Bahamas. Gaming is a major tourism asset in the Bahamas. How many places don't even have a slot machine? It took a while. It took me all afternoon to find two properties that seemed to fit our parameters: good resort, safe, reasonable price, no slots, restaurants on site. It looked like I would have to make a quick trip there to check them out.

If I hadn't worked late, I'd have missed Captain Dave's call. It was six thirty, and I almost didn't answer the phone.

'Miss Hale? Captain Dave. I had a message that you called.'

'Yeah. Thanks for calling back. Any news?'

'No. Sorry. Nothing.'

'They're still searching?'

'Yes, yes. The Coast Guard is still searching, and a lot of local boaters are out. They're communicating with the Coast Guard. There are a lot of people out there looking.'

And not finding anything. Unspoken, it hung there in the air, hummed on the line.

'Look, I know you all know how to do this. I just, I just . . . I don't know. I was just thinking, wondering, I mean, if you know where he was, when you talked to him last, and which way the current moves from there, where something would get to in a couple of days, which direction at least?' I quit rambling.

Captain Dave cleared his throat. 'I'm sorry. Yeah, you're right. Folks who know the waters, men who've been around here forever, they know how the currents go. But . . . a storm like that, winds like that . . . You can't predict. You know, with the wind, anything on the surface, there's no way to know.'

I nodded, but Captain Dave couldn't see me. 'Yeah, that makes sense,' I said finally. 'Is anything missing from the boat, besides the life jacket, I mean?'

'Oh, yeah. Most anything that would have been on deck, outside the cabin, cushions from the deck. They float, you know. They're not life jackets, but you can hold on to them. They float. He coulda' grabbed one of them, more'n one, float a long time. Some bumpers were gone, some line. The bumpers float, too.'

'What about the life raft? One was on the boat, right? Was it . . . is it still there?'

Silence. Then he spoke. 'Yeah. Yeah, there was a life raft, inflatable, fastened in a container bolted on deck. And, yeah, it's still there. The container was open, the raft partially inflated, like maybe he tried to get to it. Yeah, it's still there.'

I couldn't say anything, didn't know what to say. I nodded. He waited.

'Miss Hale?'

'Yeah,' I said. 'Yeah, I'm here. Thanks. I just, I mean, I know you guys know what to do. I just . . .'

'Yeah,' he agreed, 'I know. You keep thinking there's one more thing. And you keep hoping.'

'Yeah, thanks. Thanks.'

'We're all still hoping.'

'Thanks.'

I hung up.

I locked the door behind me as I left the office, breathing deep in the summer late-afternoon air, smelling honeysuckle even here. Even in Hillsboro Village, somewhere not far away honeysuckle was growing, languishing over a backyard fence, creeping up a telephone pole, trailing its intoxicating scent like a lady, seductive but just out of sight. I was looking forward to the drive home, late enough to miss the traffic, the Spider's top down in the soft air. But clouds were piling up in the west, darkening the sunset. The air felt heavier than it had when I was out at lunch, and I could smell the rain on it.

Then it hit me. The cat! I'd forgotten all about Rex! That's exactly why I had never wanted a pet. I didn't want to have to rush home to feed something or let it out or put it in. Now this tiny homeless cat was hungry and feeling abandoned in this strange cardboard box. I had to get home.

I raced the clouds across town, west to east, trying to beat the storm I could see coming and hoping the cat wasn't panicking. As I seemed to be.

TWENTY-TWO

The first huge raindrops were splattering against my windshield like water balloons when I pulled into the driveway. I put the top up. Lightning was punctuating the storm. I ran across the yard. As I reached the porch, lightning hit close enough to rattle the house. I heard the ripping sound of a tree splitting nearby. I jumped and dropped my keys, but I finally made it inside. I leaned against the door, glad to be in out of the storm and feeling safe.

Then I heard it. Not really meowing, more like mewing.

The cat! The poor baby had been all alone in the storm. OK. But this is why I never wanted a pet.

I followed the sound of the mewing to the kitchen. 'It's OK, baby. I'm here. It's just a little old storm. Yeah, you're fine.' I was talking to the cat. One day, and I was talking to the cat.

I picked it up, looked Lightning in the eyes. 'I am not going to talk to you. Don't be thinking you can just move in here and I'll be telling you about my day at work.' Holding him with my left arm, I emptied and refilled his water dish and set them both on the floor. He drank and then wandered back to me, stumbling and rubbing against my wet shoe. 'Oh, no, you're doing that ankle rubbing thing.' OK, OK. I put some cat food in the appropriate dish and set it near his water.

I poured myself a glass of iced tea and picked him up and carried him to the den. I sat down, and Tigger – no, absolutely too cute – settled down in my lap. He was soft. That tiny vibrating purring. I could see how people could get used to this. I turned on the TV just in time for the local news.

Fly was the lead story. Local business leader lost at sea. There was film of the boat, a close-up of the boom where the blood was – confirmed now as Fly's blood type, not enough time for DNA yet – the torn life jacket. And Captain Dave. He looked the part with a weather-bleached gray beard and faded T-shirt, and his broad As revealed his Boston background. 'He seemed to know what he was doing, had a license. But this was a heck of a storm.' He shook his head. 'We've never lost anybody yet. Everybody's still looking.'

The camera cut back to the Nashville reporter. This story was big enough that they'd sent a local reporter to Florida. 'Jeremy, the official Coast Guard position is that this is still a search and rescue mission. Everyone here is trying to be positive.' Here he shook his head, Miami sun glinting off his hair. 'But the longer searchers go without finding Franklin Young, the harder it is to remain hopeful.'

Then the story was back in Nashville. 'Young's wife, author Erika Young, spoke briefly with reporters today.' There was Erika, somber and pale in a black suit, conservative pearls, a more restrained look than she usually wore. Her two children, Fly's children, stood on either side of her. A sad, beautiful family. 'We' – she twisted a handkerchief in her hands – 'just want everyone to know how much we appreciate your concern, your prayers. We're still confident that Franklin will be found.' She put an arm around her daughter's shoulder and gripped her son's hand. 'And the men and women who are searching for Franklin, the Coast Guard, the volunteers, people who've risked their own lives to look for Franklin – thank you. You can't know how much we appreciate what you're doing.'

The clip ended, and a photo of Fly was projected over the anchor's shoulder as she spoke, somber now. 'Business analysts here in Nashville and across the country are trying to assess the effect Franklin Young's absence may have on HealthwaRx. Young's partners have issued a statement that their first concern is to find Franklin and support his family, but that the company is stable and secure. We'll keep you informed as the situation develops.'

'Bill, is the storm going to have an effect on our weather here in Middle Tennessee?'

I wasn't listening. How long would they keep searching? I realized something that felt like sandpaper was rubbing my hand. The cat. 'Fluffy?' Who'd have thought a soft little kitten's tongue would feel like four-aught sandpaper. 'Garfield?' Nope, probably trademarked.

Suddenly I had to get out of the house. The storm had ended as quickly as it had begun, leaving sunshine to finish the day. 'Sorry, Kitty, this bonding's going to have to wait.' I picked up the phone and called MaryNell. 'I really, really need a movie or something. Can you meet me?'

'Oh, hon, I can't. Melissa's got five teenage girls here. I can't leave. You want to come over here?'

'No. No. Thanks, but I don't need to be in the middle of a houseful of teenage girls.' I tried to keep the disappointment out of my voice.

'Julie's here. Sam's daughter. You could bond.'

I had already decided that bonding was what I didn't need tonight.

'No. Thanks.'

'You OK?' I could hear the concern in her voice.

'Yeah, yeah, I'm fine.'

'What?' Her voice was insistent.

'I don't know.'

'This Franklin Young thing?'

'Yeah. I just feel funky, I guess. I'm fine. I'll talk to you tomorrow.'

I took the kitten back to his box in the kitchen. 'I'll be back.' That was another reason I never wanted a pet. There I was explaining myself to a cat!

I opened the door, and the humidity hit me in the face. The heavy, damp air from the storm was hot and oppressive.

I didn't know where I was going. I just knew that I had to get out. I put the top down on the Spider. At least the air would be moving then.

I headed for Hamilton Creek. The sailboat marina on Percy Priest was one of my favorite places to escape. I found it quiet, a few sailors cleaning up, tying down, some cooking supper and preparing to sleep aboard. Fifty yards offshore, maybe a hundred yards, a breeze ruffled the surface of the water. I walked the docks, listening to the music of the halyards and the masts. Wind chimes.

I stopped to listen, nodding a greeting to a gray-haired couple packing their gear out in canvas bags, their steps matching from long years of practice. I smiled and felt . . . what? Sad? Jealous? I wanted that. Not now, maybe. But when I got to be their age, I wanted someone beside me, someone who knew me. I watched the sun fading over the masts, telltales revealing the faint breeze.

He was wrong. Fly was wrong. It wasn't 'Whiter Shade of Pale'. I remembered. It was 'Unchained Melody', and time was going by awful slowly for me.

As the sunset rose, pink and coral behind the city skyline, I walked back up the ramp to the parking lot. The sun was down, but the air wasn't cooling. The humidity was holding the day's sticky heat. I got back in the car and drove, across the dam first, then just around. The lake was dotted with lights from boats still out.

TWENTY-THREE

would have sworn I was driving aimlessly, but I found myself on Sam Davis' street. I had been to Sam's house before, but never uninvited, never dropping by without warning. And I probably shouldn't now. We had no commitments. I didn't know he wouldn't have guests or if he were even at home. I did know his daughter was at MaryNell's, though. I could have called. I had a cell phone in the car. But I didn't. I didn't know what to say.

His car was in the drive. I pulled in behind it and went up the short walk. I knocked and felt like running away before he could see me, like a kid. He opened the door wearing shorts and an old T-shirt, a glass of ice water in his hand.

'Hey. Come in.' He was glad to see me, and I needed that.

'Hey.'

'You OK?' He looked concerned.

'Maybe.'

Barefoot, in shorts and a T-shirt, Sam looked younger, the muscles in his arms and legs sculpted, not like a body-builder's but lean and hard, like a runner's, with nothing to spare. He looked at the glass in his hand. 'Want something to drink?'

'No. I don't think so.'

He nodded. 'Have you had supper?'

I shook my head.

He nodded again. 'We could have supper.'

I nodded.

'I was just cleaning my gun. You OK to wait while I finish?'

'Sure, of course.'

'You sure you're OK?' He came close to me and touched my face. I smelled the cleaning oil on his fingers. He wrapped his hand around the back of my neck and pulled me closer, then leaned down and kissed me. He stood there for a moment, looking into my eyes, his expression unreadable. 'Come on.'

He smiled. 'You can have your first lesson in cleaning and breaking down a gun.'

I followed him through the entryway into the den. The house was neat, but it looked like a man's house. I guessed very little had been changed since his ex-wife had moved out, taking what she wanted to keep, but it looked somehow womanless. Beige walls, framed prints, plaid upholstery. He moved a newspaper to make room for me to sit on the sofa beside him. Parts of a gun were spread on newspaper on the coffee table in front of us. I looked around. Photos of Julie in elementary school, Julie cheerleading, Julie's senior photo filled one wall. A collection of old metal signs and license plates, one of the few touches that seemed to reflect Sam's personality, decorated the opposite wall. A Texaco star, Coca-Cola, Purity Milk, a couple of signs for companies with Davis in the name, an old license plate from the days when Tennessee plates were shaped like the state itself.

He looked up. 'How about if I order some pizza?'

'Sure.' I didn't care. Not tonight. I probably would have forgotten supper if he hadn't mentioned it.

He picked up a cell phone lying on the coffee table and hit a speed dial number. 'Yeah, I need to order a pizza. OK.' He waited. 'No problem. Let's see, give me a large pepperoni and mushrooms, tomatoes' – he looked at me and raised his eyebrows in question – 'anchovies?' I nodded. 'Yeah, anchovies,' he continued. 'No, thanks, I think that's all.' Another pause. 'OK, sure. Thanks.' He turned to me. 'Forty-five minutes.'

Sam picked up a tool with a T-shaped handle, a metal rod and a plastic attachment. At the end of the plastic section was a slit, like an eye in a needle, only larger. He threaded a square of cotton through the slit then dipped it into a small, shallow black tray filled with a strong-smelling liquid.

'How often do you do that?' I asked.

'Every time I use it, at least. I went to the shooting range this afternoon. If I haven't shot, at least once a month. But I usually go to the range that often.' He grinned. 'Have to keep it clean.'

He picked up the steel tube from the newspaper and pushed

the tool into it, rubbing the cloth all around inside the barrel of his Glock.

'What's that?' I asked.

'Cleaning solvent. It gets the gunpowder out. Gunpowder gets all over everything. And it loosens the lead particles from bullets that stick to the inside of the barrel.' He unscrewed the plastic tip and picked up another attachment, a brush, long and thin, like a baby bottle brush but made of a wire that looked like copper. I watched while he ran the brush through the barrel, pushing it in one end, pulling it out the other, several times. Then, methodical and unhurried, he unscrewed the brush tip and replaced the plastic attachment and the handle. He threaded a clean piece of cotton into the eye and began to clean the barrel. Again and again, he dropped a soiled square of cloth onto the newspaper, threaded a clean one and repeated the task. Finally, when the cloth came out as clean as it went in, he held the barrel up, sighted through it and nodded.

'What have you been up to today?' he asked. 'Any news on Young that wasn't on TV?'

'No.' I shook my head. 'Nothing.'

He threaded another clean cloth and squeezed a drop of oil from a yellow-and-red can on the cloth that extended from each side of the eye. Outers Gun Oil, read the can. He swabbed the inside of the barrel again.

'I have a cat.'

'Oh, yeah? I thought you didn't like cats.'

'It's not that I don't like cats. I just didn't want a cat. I didn't want any pet.'

'So why do you have a cat?'

Sam picked up a cloth from the solvent pile and wiped the trigger and slide area. He wiped again with a clean cloth and then with the oil cloth patch.

'MaryNell decided I needed one. She brought me this kitten. Black and white, short hair.'

'What's its name?' He was making conversation, but his focus was on his work.

'I don't know yet. I keep trying things out, but nothing seems to fit.'

He picked up a rag and wiped the barrel and the rest of the

gun, then carefully reassembled it. He wiped the whole piece again and looked up at me.

'That's it. You do want to remember to keep the business end of the gun pointed away from you – or anybody else.' He inserted a clip.

I nodded again.

'You hope you never have to pull it out, but, when you do, you want to know it's ready, that you can depend on it to work the way it's supposed to.'

'Be prepared,' I said.

'Yep.' He put the gun into its holster and stood up to put it away in his gun safe. He came back, gathered up the soiled cloths and threw them away in the kitchen. He sat down again and packed his cleaning supplies into a wooden case fitted to hold the tins and tools and cloths. He carried the case to a cabinet and put it away. I watched as he went to the kitchen and washed his hands, scrubbing away the oil, and dried them on a paper towel. He came back, sat down beside me. He put his hand on my shoulder and rubbed my neck. 'You OK?'

I nodded, but I tucked my face into his shoulder. He wrapped his arms around me. 'So what happens when this guy does come back?' he finally asked.

I shook my head against his shoulder. 'Nothing. As far as I'm concerned. He goes home to his wife and family and buys lots of tickets from me to fly around the country making more millions.'

No one said anything for a long minute. Then the doorbell rang.

'Pizza,' Sam said as he stood. 'You want to get us some Cokes? I think there're some in the refrigerator.'

He came back into the room with a pizza as I set Cokes, plates and napkins down on the coffee table. He sat on the couch, and I settled on the floor across from him.

Sam reached for a slice of pizza, steam and anchovy scent rising from it, and took a bite. His eyes, solemn and watchful, met mine. I knew there was something he wasn't saying. I was pretty sure it was about Fly, and I was pretty sure I didn't want him to push it.

'What about you?' I asked. 'Catch any murderers today?' So I changed the subject.

He smiled. 'Not today. They're still running around loose out there. Be careful.'

Then I started talking about the kitten, filling the empty space with words, and he let me. By the time we'd run out of pizza, I'd run out of small talk. I helped clean up the debris, and there was that moment.

'Well,' I said. 'I'd better go.'

He stood in front of me, not speaking immediately. 'Is that what you want?'

Who knew what I wanted? That was the problem. 'I should get back to the kitten. Strange place, he's all alone.'

He nodded, not buying it but letting me off the hook. 'Sure.'

'Thanks for dinner.'

He smiled and nodded slowly. 'Shoulda got out the candles, I guess. Next time.'

'Next time,' I agreed. Then I drove back home to Felix, feeling both better and worse than I had when I left.

TWENTY-FOUR

A couple of days later, on Saturday, I decided it was time to take the cat to the vet.

'OK, Cheshire, it's time for you to meet the vet.' I called a vet I knew from church, and he worked me in. Just inside the door, Tabby and I found a sign with arrows pointing in opposite directions: dogs to the left, cats to the right. We went right.

The attendant at the counter greeted me with a clipboard and pen. 'Just fill this out, please.'

I was juggling Blackie, the clipboard, my purse and a pen. I sat and tried to hold the cat with my left hand while I balanced the clipboard on my knees and wrote. I noticed that everyone else's cat was in a pet carrier. I felt like the only mother who didn't get the memo about the dress code on the first day of school. I was embarrassed for myself and for Puss 'n Boots, too. I tried to concentrate on the form

My name, address, and phone number were no problem. Then we got to the hard stuff. Pet's name. I decided to come back to that later. Birthdate? I counted back six weeks from the day MaryNell had brought him to me. Close enough. He'd never know the difference. Indoor, outdoor or combination? Insurance? Were they kidding? Person responsible for payment? I guessed that would be me. Most of the rest of the questions didn't apply: previous vet, shots, diseases, allergies, general health history.

I went back to the pet's name blank.

I looked at the kitten. He looked back and tried to lick my hand with that sandpaper tongue. I didn't think I could tell the attendant that I hadn't been able to name a kitten. Sandy. I whispered it to him to try it out. 'Sandy?' He turned his head to look at me. OK. Good enough. I wrote it with confidence and took the form and clipboard back to the counter.

It wasn't long before a perky attendant opened a door beside the counter. 'Sandy?'

I stood and carried Sandy.

'Hello,' she said brightly. 'How are you, Sandy?' Sandy didn't answer. I wondered how many cats did.

The vet met us in the hallway and took Sandy from me. 'How've ya'll been doing?' He glanced at the form. 'Sandy eating OK? You feeding him dry or canned food?'

'Dry. Is that OK?'

'Sure. Either one's OK as long as he's eating.' He weighed Sandy, took blood, felt his belly and legs, looked in his ears and mouth. 'Looks good, no mites. Judy will set you up for his shots out front.'

From there we went to PetSmart where Sandy picked out a carrier, a scratching post, more food, a fountain that circulates water so it stays fresh, and a rubber mouse with space for catnip inside. 'Only one toy,' I told him. 'We're not going to get carried away.'

TWENTY-FIVE

On Monday morning, the Coast Guard called off the search. Marcella called and told me there was no reasonable hope that Fly had survived. 'The ships that are expected to be in the area are being notified. Air traffic control will be notifying pilots. They'll still be looking for him.' No one experienced in marine search and rescue, though, expected any results. 'We're putting together a memorial service for later in the week. I'll let you know the details.'

'Thanks.'

'And there are some people out who'll need to get back into town for the service. We'll need you to make arrangements for them when we know more.'

'Of course,' I said. 'Just let me know. And just so you'll know, I'll be out of the office a couple of days next week. I have to go to the Bahamas to check out some arrangements for a group. Anyone here in the office can help you, though, if you need something while I'm gone.'

Marcella said she'd send out a company email.

I made sure I knew which HealthwaRx employees were out of town, reviewed their flight reservations and made sure I had their hotel phone numbers. It was all I could do.

I wondered how I would have felt about this if I hadn't reconnected with Fly at the reunion. If I'd just seen this on the television news, not having seen Fly in twenty years. But I had, and he'd stirred up all this . . . this history. And now it was never going to be resolved. I'd never know who Fly had really grown up to be. And I'd never know how I felt about that person.

For the first time, I was glad I had a cat to go home to.

TWENTY-SIX

n Tuesday's *Tennessean*, I saw the first hints that all might not be as it had seemed in the Youngs' financial empires. The HealthwaRx initial public offering price had been twenty dollars a share, but the stock's price had quickly climbed to seventy-five. I wished I had tried to get in on that. But now some major shareholders were questioning some of the company's accounting practices. Fly had founded the company, and, with him gone, shareholders were far less confident. The remaining partners were too busy with damage control to grieve, and the man who'd been the company's chief accountant since it was founded wasn't there, either, since he'd been murdered on a Nashville street the day before my reunion. There was a photograph of the two partners, Al Evanston and George Madison, in a forced perspective in front of the sign marking the company's headquarters.

'Franklin was an essential part of this firm,' Madison was quoted as saying. 'There's no question about that. And he always will be. His vision, his creativity, his model for understanding what the market needs – and delivering that – that's what this company is all about.'

Evanston, according to the reporter, agreed. 'I suppose it's natural that shareholders would be concerned. As a publicly traded company, HealthwaRx doesn't have a lot of history. It's only been a few weeks. But we've been doing what we do for a long time. Franklin Young helped make this firm not just successful, but responsible. That's not going to change.'

Both insisted that their first priority was to help Fly's wife and children through these difficult days and ensure that HealthwaRx continued to grow.

I called Mark as soon as I'd read the story.

'Thought I might hear from you,' he said.

'That's a good thing, right?'

Mark laughed. 'Sure. What'd ya need?'

'I just wondered what's the story behind the story.'

'I don't know much for sure, just that there are some rumors of missing cash.'

'At HealthwaRx?'

'Yes, and that's the reason everybody's trying to reassure shareholders. But Erika's Lifestyle Balance, Inc., is privately held. And the word is, Erika's upset that some liquid assets aren't where she thought they were, like in the bank.'

'What's going on?'

'Nobody knows. But it looks suspicious that your buddy Fly had access to the accounts, and he was leaving the country when he died.'

'Leaving the country? He was sailing!'

'People do leave the country in boats. What was so important about that trip that he had to sail out of Miami right into the path of a storm?'

'You think he embezzled it?'

'I don't know what I think. But a lot of people are asking questions. And they're starting to ask more questions about Patton's death, the accountant, too.'

'Mark! Fly was incredibly wealthy! What would be the point?'

There was silence for a moment. 'You ever know anybody who had enough? Especially a rich man who had enough?'

I didn't have an answer for Mark, but I didn't want to believe the rumors. I couldn't believe it was true.

Fly's secretary, Marcella, called a little before lunchtime. 'There's going to be a memorial service Friday,' she said. 'Eleven o'clock, visitation beginning at ten.' She named one of the larger churches in Belle Meade. 'It'll be a crush, so you'll want to come early.'

'I saw the article in the paper. How are things going?'

'Pretty much what you'd imagine. It's a zoo. No, there's some control in a zoo. Everybody's yelling at everybody else. We're getting auditors in here. Erika's calling or she's having her assistants call. She's planning this service to say what a great husband and father Franklin was, but if he were here right now, she'd kill him. Can you make arrangements to get everybody back here? You know who's out of town?'

'Yeah, I pulled together a list yesterday. I'll get back to you this afternoon with the details.'

'Great. We're telling everyone who's traveling to contact you, so you'll probably start getting calls pretty quick.'

'I don't want you to say anything you shouldn't, but what's this I'm hearing about Erika's company?'

'I don't know. Something about missing cash, lots of missing cash, and Franklin's always been the CFO. I've worked for this man for fifteen years. I don't believe a word of it. In fact, if I hadn't seen the pictures of that storm, I'd swear Erika had a hand in all this somehow. I wouldn't trust that woman as far as I could throw her surgically reconstructed hide. And I'm getting really tired of her calls insinuating her missing assets have been buying me lingerie.'

Fly and Marcella? One more thing I didn't want to think about.

Marcella continued. Obviously, she needed to vent. 'I've worked hard for that man, for this company, and he's paid me a good salary, bonuses that let me know he appreciated the hours I put in. And I don't like that woman talking to me as if . . . as if . . .' She stopped, and I heard her take a deep breath. Silence.

'Marcella? You OK?' I heard something. A sob? Another deep breath.

'I'm sorry. It's just . . .'

'Don't apologize. I can't imagine the strain you all are under.' I thought she was crying. 'Look, I'll call you back when I have the reservations changed. And you let me know if there's anything else I can do to help.' What else could I say?

'Thanks, Campbell. I'm sorry. I shouldn't have said any of that.'

'It's OK. I'll talk to you later.'

TWENTY-SEVEN

I did manage to change the flight reservations for all the HealthwaRx employees who were out of town so they could be back in time for Fly's memorial service.

There was a crowd at the service. I entered the church behind the mayor and several state legislators. I hadn't intended to introduce myself to Erika Young. With this crowd of people who were her friends, power brokers and important business associates, my condolences would be meaningless to her. I didn't expect she had ever heard my name. I was wrong.

As I entered the church I found myself in a line leading toward Erika and her children. A woman and two men stood near her, introducing her to each visitor – or reminding her of their names. At the far end of the line stood Mrs Young, Fly's mother, and she was clearly devastated. As I drew nearer, I watched. It was a very efficient system and let Erika look gracious, helped her make each person feel valued.

I reached the woman beside Erika first. She wore an expensively cut, conservative dark suit, and her dark hair was cut neat and short. She began to introduce herself. 'Thank you for coming. I'm Marcella Andrews, Mr Young's secretary.'

'Marcella! I'm glad to meet you face-to-face. I'm Campbell Hale.'

'Campbell, of course. It's good to meet you. Thanks for everything you've done this week. You don't know how much you've helped me.'

'I was glad to be able to help. Please let me know if there's anything else I can do.'

'I will. Thank you. Have you met Al Evanston and George Madison?' She turned toward the two men. 'George, Al, this is Campbell Hale, our new travel agent. Campbell, George Madison and Al Evanston.' I'd seen the two men on television, of course, and in newspaper photos, but they looked older than

I had expected. The strain of the last couple of weeks was showing through the golf tans.

'Ms Hale. Thanks for all your help. We appreciate your getting everyone back so quickly,' Madison said.

Evanston added, 'Yes, thanks. We're a close company, family, really, so we wanted everyone to be able to be here. And thanks for coming. You and Franklin were old friends, I understand?'

'Yes, we were. I hadn't seen Fl . . . Franklin since high school, though, until recently. I'm glad, at least, that we reconnected before this.'

Madison and Evanston nodded. I realized that we had Erika's attention. I turned toward her, and Al Evanston, standing closest to her, began to introduce me. She interrupted him.

'Ms Hale. Yes, I've heard so much about you.' Something in her tone sounded as if she hadn't looked forward to meeting me. 'How kind of you to come today.' She looked perfect, the ideal advertisement for her diet and exercise lifestyle. The black cap-sleeve linen sheath fit perfectly, not a wrinkle on her or the dress. Her long, blonde hair was swept back in a simple ponytail, her only jewelry tasteful pearls, a choker and earrings.

'I'm so sorry,' I began. I used to try so hard to say the right thing to grieving family members. I had finally decided, though, that there is no right thing. Nothing I could say would make her loss less. I settled for telling her I was sorry.

'Thank you, Ms Hale. I don't believe you know my children. Cooper, Jordan, this is Campbell Hale, an old friend of your father's.'

I was efficiently passed along the line. I spoke briefly to the children, both attractive and well-mannered. I told Cooper how excited Fly had been about the planned trip to Alaska. He looked blank, but what could I expect from a teenager who had gone through what he had during the past week?

'Mrs Young, I . . .'

'Campbell.' Fly's mother reached out and hugged me. It struck me how much older she looked than the last time I had seen her. Her face was drawn; her kind eyes looked tired. 'Thank you for coming. Your parents sent the sweetest card this week. Please tell them how much it meant to me. And I'm so glad you and Franklin had seen each other again and talked. I . . .' She glanced toward her daughter-in-law and grandchildren. 'Well, you were such a good friend to Franklin.' She squeezed my hands. 'Thank you.' She seemed about to cry, and I knew I was.

I hugged her quickly and moved on. I found a seat in the back.

The service was meaningful and well planned. Both partners and the governor spoke briefly, and the minister's message was brief, personal and comforting. I watched as Fly's family left the church. I saw the pain in his mother's face and knew one person, at least, mourned him truly. Mrs Young had lost her husband and now her only son. I thought, as I watched her, how wrong that was. Mothers should not have to bury their sons.

TWENTY-EIGHT

I went back to work, of course, but I'm not sure I accomplished much. I didn't do anything that I couldn't check over the next day. I didn't trust myself.

When I got home, I was glad to find Sandy waiting for me. He didn't make me talk while I fixed his supper and mine, which I thought showed a far greater sensitivity than I had any right to expect from a kitten his age. While I forced myself to eat, he played with his catnip mouse.

I went to the closet of my guest room. On the top shelf, at the very back, was the Frye boot box that held my high school scrapbook. The scrapbook had long ago begun to come apart. It was much thicker than it was made to be, with football and basketball programs, parts of corsages, notes, prom programs, concert tickets, even, I'm sorry to admit, report cards. So when I had found a box that fit it, I'd put the whole thing in. The souvenirs of my life, my young life anyway. I try not to save the souvenirs anymore. I don't want to think of myself sitting around in my old age looking at scrapbooks instead of living. But I'd never been able to let these go. I pulled the box down and put it on the guestroom bed.

I looked through my compact discs and found some old ones, actually CD versions of the old LP albums I used to have. I loaded them into the player and settled down to remember. Sandy followed me and asked so plaintively that I picked him up and let him sit beside me.

Fly had been a part of so many of these memories. I suppose I was looking for him in the box.

There was my exhibitor ribbon from the Middle Tennessee Science Fair, my electronic handwriting analysis from what? The State Fair? It didn't say, but it said that I am, or was, frank, sociable, imaginative, cultured, optimistic and self-reliant. No wonder I saved it. The stub of a NASA tour ticket from a science club trip in my freshman year, postcards, letters.

The memories of Fly started with a football program, a bowl game in the fall of our freshman year. On the next page was a Polaroid photo of Fly and me in the stands at a basketball game. Taped below it was a paper strip from a Hershey's Kiss. The tiny writing added to it was blurred from the years, but I could make out the number 10 in front of the word 'Kisses'. A paper straw was taped to the page. What could have been the significance of an unopened straw?

A few pages over I found the letters Fly had written me the first time I'd gone to cheerleading camp. I was no more than an hour and a half from home and only there for a week, but he'd written letters. It made me smile. He'd sent money for me to come home early – $1500 in Monopoly money. Where had he gotten that stationery? Stolen from his mother? Light blue with forget-me-nots in the corner. 'This week has seemed like a month, and it's only Wednesday.' Taped to the envelope, I'd saved movie ticket stubs and a photo of Fly from elementary school. From sometime later in the year, an early hint of trouble to come from the gossip column of the school paper: 'Fly, who is it this week?' More photos. Hard to believe I had actually picked out those eyeglass frames. Play programs, crumbling flowers and fading paper streamers.

Then my sixteenth birthday party. He'd sent me the first

bouquet of roses I had ever received. I had pressed them all
– sixteen red roses and the card that came with them. 'Happy
Birthday. Love, Fly.'

That summer there were more letters written to cheerleading
camp. New stationery – roses this year. He had written that
he was sitting in his room drinking milk and protein powder
to beef up for football, listening to my favorite album because
he missed me. He'd decided that he would come to see me
and had bought a map to find the way. He had made up a
different return address for each letter that year, all from jails,
the Murfreesboro Jail, Tennessee State Prison, San Quentin,
with cell numbers. I had to laugh. Each letter told me how
much he missed me, how much he loved me, how if I didn't
hurry home he'd probably do something desperate, wind up
in jail.

The last letter had arrived after we'd left for home and had
been forwarded to my house. He'd written it when he and his
friend Mike had gotten home from their road trip to camp,
and in it he invited me to a family reunion that weekend.
'Love, Fly.' There were more photographs, ticket stubs, football
programs, then abruptly after that football game when his best
friend had given me the bad news, no more souvenirs of Fly.

I suddenly remembered the day after the game. There had
been a pickup flag football game on an empty field beside the
school. Playing football was the last thing I felt like doing
after crying most of the night and getting no sleep, but I went
anyway. That pride thing again. He never said a word to me
that day. I remember another girl who had briefly dated him
kept hitting me every time a play gave her a chance. I thought,
she doesn't know. She doesn't even know that I'm not in her
way anymore. Toward the end of the game, the ball, in a wild
punt, dented my mother's car. It was that kind of weekend.

Young love was in the souvenirs, sweet and impossibly
passionate, but I'd found the hurt and betrayal, too. The truth
seemed as hard to hold on to as the roses that crumbled when
I touched them. Love, Fly.

TWENTY-NINE

The weekend was long. MaryNell called, but I wasn't in the mood to see a suspense movie. I didn't hear from Sam, but Sandy hung in there with me.

On Monday morning a message from Marcella was already in my voicemail when I arrived at work. 'Call me, please.'

I am convinced that there is no conspiracy of top-level CEOs that run the country for one important reason. I've never met a CEO who could even run his own company without an efficient secretary. It may be more politically correct to call them administrative assistants now. I'm fine with that. I'll call them whatever they want to be called. My point is, this economy doesn't work without them. And every honest businessperson I've ever discussed this with agrees.

So, if Marcella wanted me to call, she had my attention. I called.

'Thanks for getting back to me so fast,' she said. 'I have a favor to ask.'

'Sure. What can I do?'

'You said you might be going to the Bahamas this week.'

'Yes, just for a couple of days. I'm making some arrangements for a group that's going in a few months.'

'Will you go through Miami?'

'Probably. I haven't booked anything yet.'

Marcella took a deep breath. 'Things are crazy here. This soon after going public, the COO missing. We can't spare anyone. You can imagine. We've got state auditors, federal auditors, our private auditors and everybody's lawyers crawling all over each other. And with Charles Patton gone and Franklin not here, no one knows what's going on. It's not much better at Lifestyle Balance, but at least they're privately owned. They don't have the feds and the state. Plus Erika's shooting a new video. She says it can't be put off. Too many people's schedules are involved.'

She paused to breathe. I waited. I sympathized, but I couldn't see what any of this had to do with me.

'Somebody needs to go to Miami. The boat Franklin sailed down there doesn't really matter. We can arrange for it to be sold later. But there are some personal effects that Franklin left on both boats, the one he sailed down there to be refurbished and the one he chartered, the one he was on when the storm hit. We really should have one of the lawyers go down, but they're all busy here. Beyond busy.' She paused again. 'I know this is above and beyond, but could you help?'

'Me?'

'I know it's a lot to ask, but if you're connecting through Miami, I was hoping you could go to the marina, pick up Franklin's things there. Nobody knows what kind of shape his laptop is in, but I'd sure like to see it before somebody thinks to subpoena it. Then there are probably some things on Franklin's own boat. It's been locked since Franklin left it there. Captain Dave wants a representative from the family or the company to be there when he checks it out. He's got good security there, but the sooner we deal with this the better.'

'Well, sure. I guess. What would I need to do?'

'Talk to Captain Dave. Bring the laptop and whatever's convenient with you. Ship the rest. The company will pay your way. You can stay in the company condo on the beach. I know the middle of summer isn't the best time to go to south Florida, but, if you can manage an extra day, it would help.' She paused. 'It would mean a lot to me.'

I thought fast. I did want to keep the HealthwaRx account, and, with Fly dead, I would only keep it by providing service that kept everyone happy. Marcella hadn't said it; it wasn't a threat, but I had a feeling that if I didn't do this, I could kiss this account goodbye. And it was just as easy to connect through Miami as Atlanta.

'OK. Sure. I haven't made any arrangements yet, but I'll get on that and call you back.'

'Thanks, Campbell. Everyone here will appreciate it very much.'

I hung up and looked at my calendar. In addition to appointments, I always wrote the dates for final payments, deadlines, anything I didn't want to miss. The next couple of days were busy, but nothing critical was on the book. An extra day wouldn't hurt.

I started pulling up air schedules. American flies non-stop to Miami, but generally has tougher advance payment requirements. And American no longer pays commissions to travel agents. Southwest flies non-stop between Nashville and Fort Lauderdale. Smaller airport, more flexible requirements, non-stops to Freeport, and Southwest still pays commissions. Only five percent – and that doesn't include taxes, fees and fuel surcharges – but it's something. Availability for the next couple of days looked pretty good. I talked to Lee and the others in the office. They assured me they could handle anything that might come up.

About an hour later, Erika called.

'Campbell, this is Erika Young. I want to thank you again for all you've done for us. This has been so difficult. And thank you for coming to the service, of course. Franklin would have been so touched. And his mother was so glad to see you.'

'You're welcome,' I said. 'I know this must be a terribly hard time.'

'It is. I know business is the least of our concerns now, but things must go on. There are other people to consider. I have a video shoot this week that's been scheduled for six months. I certainly don't want to do it now, but I can't put them off. There are too many other people involved.'

I was beginning to get the picture. Erika wasn't thinking of herself. Right.

She continued. 'Franklin was supposed to be in this video, and now we're having to re-script it. And everyone at both businesses is totally consumed right now. It's not something I can talk about. I know you understand.' She stopped.

If I liked her more, I'd assume she was composing herself, trying not to lose control of her emotions, but I had an idea Erika Young never lost control. I waited. When I didn't start talking to fill the space, she went on.

'Marcella just told me that you're going to Miami.' Now the edge was in her voice.

'Yes.'

'Well, that's very kind.' She didn't sound as if she thought I was kind. 'I'm sure someone will be with you while you're going through things.'

What was she saying, that she thought I'd steal something?

'Marcella said the marina owner didn't want to, ah, pack up things on his own,' I said.

'Yes, well, you'll make an inventory, of course, have him sign it. Not that I don't trust you entirely. Marcella speaks so highly of you. But the insurance companies. You know what pains they are.'

Then I got my turn to be gracious. 'I'm glad to do whatever I can to help.'

'I should do this myself, of course. It's wrong to have to send someone to bring back Franklin's personal things, but I absolutely can't get away. There's a production schedule . . . Well, it can't be helped. I do want to know what you find there, of course.' She caught herself. 'The children, Cooper and Jordan, may want to choose something their father had with him.'

'Yes. Look. I know this has been awful for you all. I'm a stranger to you. If you're uncomfortable with my doing this, I understand.'

'We don't seem to have much of a choice. I can't go. Al and George can't go. None of the other employees can be spared. This couldn't have happened at a more inconvenient time.'

How thoughtless of Fly, to die just when the new video was scheduled. And 'other employees'? I wasn't a HealthwaRx employee.

She went on. 'Just send me a list of what you find. And you'll leave your numbers with Marcella, of course. Well, I must go now. Thank you.' She was gone.

I called Marcella.

'I got a call.'

She laughed. 'I'm sorry. I didn't have time to warn you.'

'Thanks,' I continued. 'Are you sure she wants me to go?'

'Maybe not, but she doesn't want to go herself.'

'And I'm the lesser of evils? I've checked air schedules.

I can go this afternoon, tomorrow morning. What do I need
to do?'

She gave me the address of the condo and of Captain Dave's
marina. She would call ahead, have a key waiting for me. I
should charge my ticket to HealthwaRx, rent a car, and bill
them for all my expenses.

'I guess bring back whatever you find that's personal. Ask
Captain Dave to help you arrange to have anything big shipped
back. If things get much stickier around here, the boat and
whatever's on it may be impounded. I think Erika wants everything personal off before that. And bring me Franklin's laptop
if it's there. I'd appreciate it if you didn't say anything about
that to anyone for the time being. We'll do a letter of author-
ization. I'll fax a copy over to you in the next few minutes.'

'OK. I expect I'll have questions. I'll call you.' I wouldn't
mind seeing that laptop myself. I wasn't sure I wanted all the
lawyers in Nashville to see that last email Fly had sent me. I
didn't want to have to explain that.

'Sure. And, Campbell, I really do appreciate this. The
partners will, too.'

'No problem. I'll be in touch.'

I made a reservation for an afternoon flight and called the
properties in Freeport that I needed to inspect. I called and
left a message for Captain Dave with the condo phone number
and that I'd probably be in to see him on Wednesday. I went
home just before lunch, packed, took Sandy to MaryNell and
made it to the airport in plenty of time to make it to
Fort Lauderdale and on to Freeport that night. I was on the
plane before I realized that I hadn't said anything to Sam
about going. I couldn't decide how I felt about that.

Any other time, I'd have enjoyed spending a few days in
Freeport. With relatively inexpensive charters and ever easier
access even to islands that were once remote in the Caribbean,
the Bahamas don't seem as exotic as they used to. People have
been to the Bahamas, as if they're checking off a list. Now
it's time to do St Bart's or St Lucia. I like the Bahamas. I like
the color, the feel, the people. If I want to spend some time
on a beach, it's nice not to have to spend all day flying and
changing planes to get there. But there was too much going

on this time. With a little luck, I could check out both resorts, talk to both sales managers and fly back to Fort Lauderdale by the next night.

For once, luck was with me. I toured both properties, taking lots of photographs with my phone so I could forward them easily, had breakfast at the first, a late lunch with fresh seafood at the second, talked with staff at both and made the airport in plenty of time to catch an early evening flight back to Florida.

THIRTY

I had thought July in Nashville was hot and humid. I picked up the rental car keys and went outside into the open air steam bath that is south Florida in the summer. Everything I had on stuck to me, and my hair went limp and straight. I turned the air conditioner on high and adjusted the vents to dry the sweat trickling down my neck. I headed south from Fort Lauderdale toward Miami as the sunset faded.

I knew I was taking the long way, but the ocean is the only justification for Florida. I took the Sheridan exit off I-95 east to A1A and one of America's great drives. I cruised the beaches from Hollywood south, the T-shirt and shell shops crowded up against exclusive high-rise condominiums, luxury hotels next to tiny mom and pop motels that still hung on like souvenirs of the fifties.

Just past South Beach, I saw the sign for Captain Dave's marina. I slowed down but didn't turn in. It certainly wasn't the glitziest marina I'd passed. It had the look of a serious, working boatyard. The sign advertised a dry dock, security and year-round maintenance.

The HealthwaRx condominium was just a couple of miles farther south. It was an older building, ten floors, art deco architecture and the look of recent renovation. I pulled into a semi-circular drive and parked in front of the door.

Inside, a manager, Cuban-American and immaculate in

linen slacks and a polo embroidered with the condo's logo, greeted me, told me that Marcella had called and insisted that I call him if I needed anything. He told me how distressed he and the entire staff had been to hear of Mr Young's death. It was a corporate property, so clients, employees would have stayed there at various times, but Fly and the other partners had been there enough to get to know the permanent staff.

The manager pointed out the way to the beach and the pool. He told me where I could park, in the lot in front or in an underground garage.

'Did Mr Young stay here before he went out?'

'Yes, he did. He was here for one night. Two of our staff went out with the volunteers to search for him.'

'Did you talk to him? Was he aware of the storm?'

He shook his head. 'We didn't talk about that, but that storm took an unexpected turn west. The original forecast was that it was headed more northerly. If he didn't hear a corrected weather report, he might not have known until it was too late to get out of the way.'

Yes, but why wouldn't he have followed changes in the weather forecast? He certainly had all the technology to know the minute conditions changed.

The manager gave me an electronic key to the HealthwaRx condo on the second floor. 'You'll need that key to enter any door except the property's front one,' he said, 'and it's manned twenty-four hours a day. This key also allows you to re-enter the grounds and pool area from the public beach.

'The unit was cleaned after Mr Young was here,' he continued, 'but it will be cleaned daily while you're here.' After Marcella had called, the kitchen had been stocked with basics. If I wanted anything else, the management offered a shopping service. If I called before ten, groceries would be delivered by four. I didn't think I'd be there long enough to need more groceries.

'I'll have Cesar take your bags up to the unit. Would you like me to show you the way?'

'No, thanks. I'm sure I can find it.'

He pointed the way to the parking area and the elevator. As

I went out the door, Cesar, I presumed, came in carrying my luggage. It wasn't much; I had packed light.

I parked in the basement garage and rode up the elevator past the lobby to the second floor. Off the elevator, I turned to the left and found 207. I unlocked the door, went inside and closed it behind me. My bags were sitting just inside. Across a large sitting room, I faced a wall of glass that overlooked the ocean and pool. Heavy drapes were pulled back on each side, with sheers covering the glass. I followed a light to the kitchen. Two bottles of wine, one red and one white, bread, cereal and a bowl of fruit were on the counter. I opened the refrigerator to find fresh orange juice, grapefruit juice, milk, butter, jam, sandwich meats, lettuce, bottled water and soft drinks.

I walked over to the sliding doors that centered the wall of glass and opened onto a wide balcony that seemed to run the length of the unit. I stepped out onto the balcony. The air hung heavy and muggy, but I smiled as I breathed in the sea smells.

I leaned against the rail, looking beyond the gardens and pool below to the surf crashing softly on the beach. Until a few weeks ago, I hadn't seen Fly Young in years, decades. That was OK. I had a good life without him. Then he was back, stirring everything up. Now I was standing in his beach condominium, and he was dead.

I'd joked with Mark about being another person, but I wondered. Who would I have been if Fly and I had stayed together? Who knows? Would I have had the independence, the confidence, occasionally, at least, that I had if I'd married Fly? The more I thought about it, the more I doubted it. I hadn't when we dated. Of course, I was seventeen then. But I always seemed to be worried about what he thought, whether he was attracted to someone else. With good reason. Who would I have been after twenty years of that? And, if what Fly had said and hinted to me was anything to judge by, Fly really hadn't changed. Maybe that was part of why Erika was so tough and hard-shelled. Maybe it was defense. Maybe I'd have been that way, too. Or maybe I wouldn't have been strong enough. Maybe I wouldn't have any identity left. Maybe I would have disappeared.

I turned and went back inside, closing the door to keep the heat and humidity out. I wandered around, wondering how much Fly and Erika had had to do with the condominium's décor. The room's colors were soft; they wouldn't compete with the view. They were the colors of sand and the sky and the sea. Tan upholstery on the larger pieces, the large seating unit that faced the windows. Accents were soft, pale blues and greens. Prints and paintings on the walls were of boats and the sea. As I faced the front door with the ocean behind me, the dining table was to my left at the edge of the large sitting area. It had a Caribbean feel with mahogany and woven seats. The kitchen was beyond it against the front wall. One door opened to a laundry area, another to a storage closet. A short hallway led to the left; another led to the right from the sitting area.

I went to the left first and found myself in the master bedroom, which was almost as large as my house. A king-size bed covered in sea blue-green was hung with mosquito netting. The colors of the room looked like the sea, and I had a sense of being under water. It was cool and calming. Two wicker chairs and a small table were in front of large windows. An armoire stood open with a large television inside. I opened the door into a huge bathroom with a sunken tub big enough for a small dinner party. More water shades, a separate glass-walled shower, two sinks and a bidet. Two more doors opened to a linen closet and the toilet. A used towel was in a basket on the floor of the linen closet. The cleaning service must have missed that. That small sense of imperfection was somehow comforting, a touch of reality.

I didn't think I could sleep in the master bedroom, in the bed where Fly and Erika had presumably slept. That was just a little too weird. I retraced my steps and went down the other hall. Three more bedrooms opened off the short hallway. The largest was against the front wall and had no windows. It opened to a bath, large with a whirlpool tub and separate shower but less luxurious than the master bath.

I couldn't sleep in Fly's bed, but I sure wasn't going to come down here doing errands for his company and not wake up to an ocean view. Across the hall were two rooms, still roomy if smaller than the other one. Each had a full wall of glass facing the sea. A smaller Jack and Jill bathroom joined the two rooms.

I chose the one nearer the living area, a soft coral pink, sunset colored room. I went back to the front door to get my bags and put them in the room. There were no personal photographs. I wondered if the condo were rented out sometimes. I felt sure that clients and employees used it. It wasn't quite as impersonal as a luxury hotel room, but almost. I don't know exactly what I'd hoped to find, what I'd hoped to learn about Fly and his life here, but I hadn't found it.

I closed the drapes in the bedroom and undressed. I kicked off my shoes and hung my blue linen slacks and tunic in the closet. I put on shorts and a T-shirt and went back to the kitchen. I took a bottle of water from the refrigerator and an apple from the bowl on the counter. As I opened the doors that opened from the living room to the balcony, I realized that I hadn't locked the doors when I had closed them before. I hadn't locked them because I hadn't unlocked them in the first place.

I suddenly felt insecure in this strange place, vulnerable, knowing it had been unlocked. It was a second-floor balcony, of course, but I saw as I looked out that any half-committed burglar could climb up from the garden and pool area. A sturdy tree came close. A short leap could get you across the gap. I decided to check the other doors.

The front door was locked, of course, but doors opened to the long balcony from three of the four bedrooms, the master, the room I was in and the room on the other side of the Jack and Jill. With the living room doors, that made four openings to the balcony. All four were closed but unlocked. I locked them as I went. I had trouble with the master bedroom door. The tab that controlled the lock didn't want to move. I pushed, then opened the door to feel the lock itself and found that it had been taped. Just like the door to the Watergate complex, a simple piece of tape kept the lock from engaging.

Leaving the doors unlocked hadn't been an oversight. Someone had wanted to make sure that these doors weren't locked. An employee setting up a burglary? I had lost my appetite.

I called the manager's desk.

'Would you like me to have someone come up and make sure the doors are secure?' the night manager, Manuel, asked.

'No, I guess not,' I said. 'I've locked them now. I just thought I should report it.'

'Of course. Thank you. The grounds are patrolled. I'll talk with the security staff. No one should have access to the grounds without a key. The electronic key that opened your front door also opens the gate from the beach. The grounds themselves are fenced.'

I accepted his assurance. But I still felt uneasy. Someone wanted to be able to get into this condominium without walking in the front door and without a key. Like my daddy used to say, if you've got to be out after midnight to do it, it can't be good. Maybe it wasn't exactly like that, but, if you had to break in to do it, it couldn't be good.

I walked back through the condominium again. What was there to steal? A lot of money had been spent on decorating, but there wasn't anything that could be sold easily for a lot of money or much that was portable. Expensive linens, yeah, but what's the market for that? What would be the point?

A towel was on the floor in the master linen closet. Wrapped guest soaps were beside each sink, tub and shower – except in the master bath. There, one soap was unwrapped, used. I went to the bed and pulled down the covers. The bed was neatly made, and the sheets were crisp.

I looked for the most fragile glasses I could find and put them in front of all the doors. It might not stop anyone, but maybe I'd hear the breaking glass – or a yelp of pain.

I went back through the condo, looking for more signs that someone had been there since the last cleaning. I couldn't tell. I'd never been here before. I didn't know what normal was. My life had come to this: I was Goldilocks. Someone had been sleeping in Papa's bed and left a hair behind on the pillow?

THIRTY-ONE

I didn't think I'd be able to sleep at all, but I was really tired. I went to bed in the sunset room but sat up, propped against pillows where I could see both the door to the balcony and the door to the hallway. I kept listening for the sound of breaking glass. The last time I remembered looking at the clock beside my bed was two fifteen. I spent a lot of time thinking about the lanky detective and his Glock. Dear Sam, wish you were here.

I woke early from the sunlight streaming in my windows. My eyes burned and my head hurt from too little sleep. I got up, poured myself some grapefruit juice and collected my makeshift burglar alarms. None of them had been disturbed. I pulled on a T-shirt and shorts and took my juice out onto the balcony to a table and chairs. I put my feet up. This morning, sitting in the sun with the surf below me, last night's fears seemed silly. I hated feeling foolish.

I was about to dismiss the whole thing when I remembered the tape over the master bedroom lock. That wasn't my imagination. I looked around the balcony and the ground beneath it. I was only on the second floor. It wouldn't be easy to get from the ground to the balcony, but it wouldn't be impossible. I thought I could do it. I wouldn't want to try, but I thought I could.

I went inside and called the manager. I started to explain, but he stopped me. 'Manuel told me about your concerns. I'll be up immediately.'

And he was. 'I trust nothing disturbed your rest last night?' he asked.

I didn't mention my security system. 'No, everything was quiet. I . . .' How could I do this without making the maid feel attacked? 'I'd really like to talk to the housekeeper, whoever would have been in the room last.' I hurried as I saw the manager beginning to look defensive. 'I just want to talk to her.'

'I assure you, Ms Hale, our staff is very professional. Even our housekeeping staff.'

'I'm not trying to imply that they're not.' I was using my most conciliatory voice. 'It wouldn't make sense for your staff to have left the doors unlocked. There's nothing there to steal now. Your housekeeper has a key. She wouldn't need to leave a second-floor balcony door open. Please. I'd just like to talk to her.' I watched his face as he considered the implications of what I'd found. Finally he nodded.

'I'll find out who actually cleaned the unit. I'll have her come to see you. Will you be in for the next couple of hours?'

I assured him that I would as he left. Then I fixed myself some breakfast.

I was just bringing my dishes in from the balcony when the doorbell buzzed. The manager stood there with a woman about my age. She looked proud, offended and defensive, and I knew it was not going to be easy to convince her to talk to me.

'Come in. Come in. And thank you.'

She nodded briefly. '*Sí.*'

'I suppose you know why I was concerned, why I asked to talk to you. I think someone was in the condominium after you cleaned it. You're the only one who could help me figure out what happened.'

She nodded again. I couldn't tell how much she had actually understood.

'When was the unit cleaned last?'

She pulled a notebook from her pocket, flipped through and found the date: the morning after Fly had left.

I thought. 'Look, why don't we walk around. You tell me if anything looks out of place to you.'

She nodded. I gestured down the hall to the three bedrooms. She moved toward the doorway. The manager and I followed.

She moved slowly through each room. When she stepped into the room I had slept in, I said, 'I stayed in here last night. Of course, it's messed up.'

She raised her eyebrows and moved on.

In the windowless room, she walked around the room, into the bath, looking into closets, cabinets. She didn't pause until she came back into the room. She frowned slightly. She pulled back the coverlet on the bed and frowned again. She turned to the manager and spoke in rapid Spanish, shaking her head. He listened, then turned to me. 'She says she always tucks the sheet into the mattress, very precise, always the same way. You see how that sheet is, wrinkled, not tucked neatly.' He shrugged.

We followed as she went back to the living room, looked around the kitchen and spoke to the manager. He answered, then summarized for me. 'She said the refrigerator, of course, had no food in it. I explained that the food was brought in yesterday for you.' I nodded.

We went on to the master bedroom. She looked around, inspected the bed, looked into the closet, then went into the bath. She spoke again in Spanish to the manager. He raised his hands and shrugged, then turned to me. 'She said she cleaned the morning Mr Young left. She said the toilet paper is wrong now, not folded to a point, and the soap has been used, but perhaps you did that.'

I shook my head. 'No. That's how I found it.' She understood. I waited as she opened the linen closet door. She pointed and spoke intensely, shaking her head. I didn't need a translator to understand that she hadn't left the towel there. I nodded. '*Gracias*.' There. My Spanish vocabulary, along with what I needed to understand a menu.

They followed as I walked to the balcony door. I opened it and pointed to the bits of tape still sticking to the edges of the lock. 'See?'

They both looked shocked. There was more conversation in Spanish, most of which involved the housekeeper shaking her head forcefully and shrugging.

I interrupted. 'Would you ask her for me, would she normally go around and check all the balcony doors?'

He translated my question. She shrugged and shook her head. I didn't understand all of her answer, but I understood no. All that told us was that we had no idea how long the doors had been unlocked.

The manager assured me that he would have security staff watch the unit. I decided that whoever had done this needed unlocked doors to get in, so I should be safe if I locked them.

Before I went out, though, I set my own burglar alarms. I'd learned them from old spy movies, the kind where the hero trusts no one. I pawed through my cosmetic bag for a travel-size scented powder. I lightly dusted door and drawer handles. Then I pulled several of my longest blonde hairs. Individually, they were virtually invisible. I positioned at least one on each door. Anyone opening a door to the balcony would have to dislodge a hair. I saved one for the hallway entry. For good measure, I balanced one across the refrigerator door handles. Don't tell me all those hours in front of the TV were wasted.

THIRTY-TWO

Walking out into the midday Miami heat was like walking into a wall. It had that kind of force. I didn't have far to go from the door to the white rental car, but any shower-fresh feeling was gone before the air conditioning began to cool off the car. I wanted to get this over with and go home.

Captain Dave's was not far, maybe a mile, mile and a half. In another climate I might have walked it. It wasn't hard to tell that I wasn't in Nashville anymore. Bikini-topped, short-shorted girls skated by, easily doubling the speed I was making in city traffic. Same-sex couples held hands as they strolled and window shopped. Shop windows openly advertised things folks would giggle about in Nashville. I pulled into the marina parking lot and felt I was back in a world I understood.

Captain Dave's had a blue-collar feel. Boats were rocking gently at a short pier; others were out of the water, their keels awkward in dry dock. Power tools made noise, sanders and air compressors hard at work. I looked around and found a small, weathered shack that looked like it might be the office. No one paid any attention to me as I crossed the lot.

I opened the door to a single room. An aging, overworked, window air conditioner tried against all odds to make a differ-ence in the temperature. Captain Dave looked up from a desk

layered with papers so deep that some of them had yellowed.
An iMac sat on one corner like a stylized sea bird.

'Help ya?'

'I'm Campbell Hale. From Nashville. For the Young family.'

Captain Dave stood and came around his desk, extending
his hand as he reached me. 'Ms Hale. I'm sorry.' He
shook his head. 'It's the first time anything like that's happened
to one o' my boats, one o' my clients. It's hit us all hard.'
Boston was still there in his broad As.

'Thank you. It's been hard for everyone who knew Fly to
take in.'

'Fly?'

'Mr Young. Old high school nickname. His initials.
F. L. Y.'

He nodded. 'He seemed the kind of guy you'd want around
you if something went wrong.'

I nodded. What was there to say?

'Well, let me show you to Mr Young's boat. You'll be wanting
to look it over.'

Captain Dave, Dave O'Guinn, he told me, led me to the
boat I'd last seen bobbing beside the Blue Moon in west
Nashville. In spite of everything, I'd have been less surprised
to see Fly pop out of the hatch of the *Manana* at that moment
than I had been that night by the river.

We stopped on the pier beside the boat. Captain Dave turned
to me. 'You ready for this?'

I wasn't sure. I hadn't expected the lurch in my stomach at
the prospect of collecting Fly's things. I nodded. 'Yeah.'

He stepped over the rail into the well of the deck and held
out a hand to me. I grasped it, instantly aware of the strength
in that arm. I stepped across and waited for the boat to steady.

'They're going to sell this boat?' he asked.

'I think so. That's my understanding anyway. Mr Young's
secretary said the lawyers could handle that later, I think.'

'Sooner the better. We don't have much space here. I could
broker it for 'em if they want.'

I nodded. I could see what he meant. Nearly every slip was
taken.

'Already had one offer, as a matter of fact. An agent making an offer for an out-of-state buyer, he said, all cash. Guy wants it fitted up, pretty much like Mr Young wanted it, but I haven't done anything to it, won't till I hear from Mrs Young.'

Captain Dave unlocked the cabin, and I followed him down the narrow steps. It took a minute to adjust to the relative darkness of the cabin. I looked around. 'Has anyone been in here?'

Captain Dave visibly drew himself up. 'No. Nothing's been disturbed.'

'I wasn't implying that there would have been anything wrong with that. It just seems so neat, everything put away. Maybe that's what he's like anyway, but it seems almost as if he didn't expect to come back.'

He shrugged. 'Sailors tend to be that way, I guess. Shipshape, you know.' He smiled slightly. 'If things are secured, they're less likely to go flying around in rough seas.'

I nodded. 'I guess.' This was not the boat Fly had been on in the storm. This was the *Manana*, the boat he'd sailed from Nashville, leaving here to be refitted with all the new technological and navigational gadgets, the boat that held his dreams.

I started opening drawers in the galley area, but all I saw were utensils, dishes, candles, things that belonged with the boat, nothing personal. In storage lockers under the seats there were life jackets, flotation cushions, rope, nautical accessories. I moved through the galley to the forward cabin.

I took a deep breath, and I could smell him. I don't know if it was aftershave, fabric softener, shampoo or soap, but it was Fly. If time is a dimension, then was Fly's presence here on this boat as real as my own? Enough. I needed to do what I was there for and get out of town, back to Nashville and my own little house, back to Sandy.

I started opening cabinets and drawers.

The first drawer I opened had a yellow legal pad and pens. The name, address and phone number of Captain Dave's marina were on the top sheet. An estimate from Captain Dave underneath it itemized expected repairs and costs.

I found clothes, a few books: Randy Wayne White, Robert Parker, a couple of guidebooks to the Bahamas and the Caribbean, a Bible. A chart was marked with his trip from the mouth of the Tennessee–Tombigbee waterway. There was a leather ship's log with records of the trip from Nashville as well as his Gulf crossing. I found the entry for the night I'd seen him at the Blue Moon. It gave the beginning and ending latitudes and longitudes and a note:

> Departed Harbor Isle, noon; navigated Old Hickory Lake, Cumberland River & locks; docked Rock Harbor marina, 8 p.m., dinner @ Blue Moon with Campbell Hale, Sam Davis.

The log ended with his arrival here at Captain Dave's.

I found a duffel and put the clothes and log into it. I added the books, some CDs and DVDs I found. No player; he must have played them on his laptop. Captain Dave sat in the galley and made an inventory as I called out items. I went to the door. 'Was Mr Young's computer on the other boat?'

'Yes.' He nodded. 'It was pretty banged up and wet, but it was there. We have his personal items from that boat in a box over in the office. There wasn't much.' He looked apologetic. 'Some charts, a couple of books, the computer, a few clothes, toiletries, stuff like that. Everything was pretty wet.'

'What about his wallet?'

He shook his head. 'No. Must have had it in his pocket.'

I thought. 'That seems odd. On a boat, when you didn't expect to see anyone, much less buy anything.'

He shrugged. 'Habit? If he had time, he might have thought about needing identification. When he was found.'

'I guess.'

It looked to me as if he'd cleaned up on the *Manana*, leaving it ready for repairs, with only a few personal items to pack up when he got back from the charter. Even the refrigerator and head were clean.

I put the charts and yellow pad in the duffel and went back through the boat, opening drawers and storage lockers. Everything that was left seemed to be equipment, a tool kit, first-aid kit. I turned back to Captain Dave.

'Looks like this is it.'

He nodded. He looked over the list and held it out to me.

'You want to sign this?' I took his pen and signed it. He continued, 'I'll make you a copy and give you the other stuff.'

Captain Dave locked the cabin as we left and carried the duffel back to his office. Inside again, I wondered if the air conditioner's cool was worth its noise. He went around his desk, sat down and jiggled the mousepad of his computer. The screen came to life; the wallpaper on his monitor showed sculling boats on the Charles River. He found the file he wanted, clicked, and his printer began to hum. He stood.

'That's the list of his stuff that was salvaged from our boat. You'll want to look through it and make sure it matches.' He pulled a cardboard box, maybe eighteen inches by twelve by eight or so, flaps folded over each other to keep it closed. Not much. He opened the box. That's when it hit me. It must have shown on my face.

'Are you OK? Want to sit down a minute?'

I didn't answer for a second or two. I was not going to cry here.

'Hey,' he said. 'This isn't easy. Have a seat there behind my desk.' It was the only chair in the room. 'I'll get you a drink.'

I didn't want to, but I took his advice as he left the shack. I stumbled around the desk and sat down. I thought about putting my head between my knees. Was this how fainting felt? I would not faint. It was the heat, I told myself.

Captain Dave was back almost immediately with a Coke from the machine outside the door. He popped it open and held it out to me. 'Here. Drink this. Just sit there a minute. You'll be OK.'

I drank. I sat. I breathed. After a few minutes I reached for the list Captain Dave had printed out and stood up to look into the box. The laptop, more clothes, everything stiff and crusted with salt. I compared the contents with the list and signed it.

Dave took both lists to his ancient, wheezing copier and made copies. He gave a set to me. I asked him to fax a set as Erika had asked. I couldn't exactly ask him to take the laptop off the list, but I'd make sure Marcella had it first. 'I'll put this stuff in your car,' he offered.

'Thanks.' I led the way to the rental car, opening the office door, then the trunk, ahead of him. He put the duffel and box inside.

'Is there anything else I can do to help?' he asked.

I shook my head. 'Thanks. Just keep an eye on the boat until the lawyers can do whatever they need to do so that it can be sold.'

He nodded. 'I'll let people know it's going to be on the market. It's a good boat, ought to sell pretty fast if they price it reasonably. If that guy with the cash comes back, I'll call.'

'I'm sure they'd appreciate that.' I looked around. 'I, uh . . . Would . . .' I took a deep breath and started over. 'I'd like to see the boat he was on. Is it here?'

He looked surprised. 'Sure. Yeah. It's here. You can see it. If you're sure you want to.'

I nodded. 'Yeah. Please.'

He nodded and turned, leading me back toward the water. We walked onto the gangway leading to the pier. The wooden pier rocked with our steps.

Captain Dave stopped at the last boat on the left and gestured. 'This is it.'

It looked so solid, gleaming and bobbing in the water. The boom swung slightly as the small waves rocked the boat. A sail cover hid the boom from view, but I wondered where Fly's blood had been, wondered morbidly and unreasonably if any trace of it remained. If he'd seen it, if he'd dodged the boom as it swung wildly in the storm, would he be alive today? I stepped back and turned to Captain Dave. 'OK. Thanks. I know Mr Young's family appreciates your help. Thanks.'

He put out his hand to shake mine. 'I'm sorry.'

'I know. Thanks.'

He stood there as I went back to dry land, back to the car.

I turned the air conditioner on full blast and adjusted the vents to blow straight on my face. My head hurt.

THIRTY-THREE

The sun was low as I drove back to the condominium. I had done what they had sent me to do. I would find a restaurant with great fresh seafood for dinner. Tomorrow morning I would walk on the beach, swim in the beautiful pool, lie in the shade of palm trees. I would take a shower and catch a late afternoon flight home. Then I would go on with my life.

I got out of the car into the Miami heat. I shouldered the duffel and took the laptop out of the box. The box itself I left in the trunk.

I nodded to the manager, busy on his phone, on my way to the elevator. Upstairs, in the condo, I set the laptop and duffel on the dining table. Then I remembered to check my home-made burglar alarms.

Too late for the front door. I went to check the others.

Every handle was wiped clean. Everything was securely locked, but no hairs, no powder, not even on the floor. I went back to the kitchen to call housekeeping and see if the condo had been cleaned while I was out. On the pad beside the phone was a note, block letters printed in pencil: *Did you look behind the forward port bulkhead?* A strand of hair lay across it like a dare.

I froze. Someone was in the condo. No, I tried to think calmly, I had just been through the entire place. I hadn't searched closets and I really didn't want to, but I'd been in every room, checking doors. No one was here now.

I went back through the condominium, looked at my bags. I was convinced my bags had been searched. There was nothing I could put my finger on, but I felt my stuff didn't look the way I'd left it. I couldn't tell that anything was missing, though.

Why would a burglar leave me a note? What sense did that make? Whoever had been here knew why I was in Miami and wanted me to find something on Fly's boat. On one of the boats, anyway. Someone was trying to communicate with me. Where's a medium when you need one? What was that – automatic writing, a spirit writing messages to communicate with the living. Fly? I'd heard strange stories of communication from people who died at sea. Who knows?

No. OK, maybe. But I could not believe that Fly's ghost was writing me notes. Somebody, some *body* had been in here while I was gone and left this note. So far, I had no reason to think that whoever that was wanted to hurt me. He or she just wanted something retrieved from the boat. OK. I had no idea what it was, but now I wanted to see it myself. I tore the note from the pad, stuck it in my pocket and started to call Captain Dave. I hung up before I dialed the last number.

Someone knew more than I did about what was going on here. The least I could do was try to level the playing field. I'd go back and look, but I wouldn't call from here. So much for my leisurely dinner.

I didn't want to leave the things from the boat here while I was gone. What to do? Leave them with the manager? A total stranger? I decided to take them with me. Once again I balanced the duffel on my shoulder and carried the laptop. I went back out into the heat and put everything in the trunk. My camera was still there where I'd left it in the trunk. At least nothing would be visible in the car. As I got into the car and pulled into the street, I wondered who was watching.

I used my cell phone to call and make sure Captain Dave was still there.

'Yeah, sure,' he said. 'I'll be here.'

And he was, standing outside his office when I pulled in. He walked over just as I opened the door.

'Did we miss something?' he asked.

'I don't know, but I want to find out.' I told him about the note. I didn't know if I could trust Dave or not, but I couldn't have access to the boat without his cooperation.

'Hang on a second.' He went back inside his office and came back with a couple of screwdrivers. 'We'll see if this does it,' he said, holding the tools up.

We made our way back to Fly's boat, and I waited while Captain Dave unlocked the cabin.

'José!' he yelled. A man across the yard looked up. Captain Dave jerked his head, and José started toward us. '*José! Quédate alli! Quedar a la espera!*'

'It doesn't hurt to be careful,' he said in answer to the question on my face. 'Something pretty weird is going on. You're here representing the owners, so whatever's on this boat, you're entitled to take. But I don't like this, and I'm gonna feel better with somebody I trust watching our backs.'

In the forward cabin, Captain Dave crawled across the built-in bunk to the bulkhead that made the left side wall of the cabin. He went to work with a Phillip's head screwdriver, removing barely visible screws and handing them back to me. When he had one panel loose, he lifted it out to reveal a space. There, hanging on a nail projecting from the side of a support, was a canvas briefcase, identical, except for the crusted salt, to the one that had been on the chartered boat. He pulled it out, hefted it and said, 'Your note writer knew what he was talking about.' He handed it across to me.

'There's a lock,' I said as I saw the key lock sealing the two zipper pulls of the main compartment.

'Yeah.' Dave was feeling around in the space accessible from the opening. 'Think I ought to take the rest of this bulkhead apart?' He pulled a flashlight from his pocket and shone it around inside. 'I don't see anything.'

'How far can you see?'

'Pretty much from the bow to where the built-in cabinets start.'

'Then, no, I don't think you need to tear it apart. Looks like we've got what he wanted us to find.'

'Now what?'

'I take it back to Nashville.'

He nodded and stood there a moment. 'Like to know what's inside.'

'Yeah, me, too.' Silence. 'OK. I'll look through the stuff I took earlier. See if there are any keys.'

He nodded.

'You could help.'

'All right.' He smiled.

As we crossed the yard, Dave yelled to José. 'Thanks, José.' He waved. 'You can go on home now.'

We carried the canvas briefcase, the duffel and the box into Captain Dave's office. For the first time, he looked apologetic as he looked around for a surface we could put things on.

'Hang on a second,' he said. He set the box he had been carrying on the floor, then cautiously lifted several stacks of papers from his desk and put them on the floor, carefully following some system of organization known only to him. 'OK,' he announced when he had cleared about half the desk. He set the box on the desk. I dropped the duffel and briefcase to the floor. He looked up and grinned through his beard. 'I guess this is your job.'

I nodded and opened the box. This was all stuff I had seen before, no surprises, but I looked through everything again, trying to find a key or a clue. I turned pockets inside out, opened Fly's toiletries bag, held his razor, his deodorant. I looked in zipped compartments. I found condoms and wondered if he'd packed them for this trip, this trip without his wife, or if he always kept some in his bag. But no key. I opened his laptop case and checked every crevice. Captain Dave rechecked everything right behind me. I looked up. 'Nothing here.'

'Nope,' he agreed.

I repacked the box, and he set it on the floor. He replaced it with the duffel. As he watched I repeated the process. Pockets, shoes, anything that could hold anything. I even flipped through the pages of the yellow legal pad I'd found on Fly's boat. No key. I did notice a number written near the top of the last page. I wouldn't have seen it if I hadn't flipped through the pad that way. Too long for a phone number. But it didn't help us get into that briefcase. Finally, I looked up at Captain Dave. He shrugged.

'It could have been damaged, I guess,' he suggested. 'Torn open, maybe.'

I hesitated. 'No.'

'Yeah,' he agreed with obvious regret. 'I guess not.'

'I couldn't do that.'

'No. You're right.' I zipped the duffel closed. Neither of us said a word, each of us waiting for the other to come up with an idea. Neither of us did. I lifted it, started to feel around the sides, trying to feel the shapes of whatever was inside.

Like a kid shaking a Christmas present, I felt the canvas briefcase, gently shaking it, listening for rattles, trying to gauge the size and weight of the contents. There were a few small items. Keys? Coins? The bulk of the contents seemed to be rectangular solids, about the size of . . . a dollar bill? Of a stack of dollar bills? Several stacks of dollar bills?

I looked up at Dave, his eyes locked on mine. I handed the case over to him. His hands, bigger, stronger, closed over the shapes inside. He never took his eyes off me, but his face changed. He nodded, speculating but not aloud.

'I'll help you get this stuff to your car.' He lifted the duffel and the box, leaving me the briefcase. I followed him out the door, leaving the wheezing air conditioner to its task. He stopped at the car, propping the box against the rear fender as I unlocked the trunk. 'Somebody'll be in touch about the boat?'

'Yeah. They're a little preoccupied right now, but yeah. You have Marcella's number? Mr Young's secretary?'

'Yeah.'

'Thanks for your help with this.'

'Sure.'

'And if you should happen to be around either of those boats and find a key . . .'

He grinned. 'I'll let you know. When are you leaving?'

I was booked on a flight back to Nashville the next afternoon. I told him the time, made sure he had the phone numbers at the condominium, my cell number, my office. 'I missed dinner. Is there someplace good around here? Fresh seafood?'

He thought a second. 'Yeah, sure. The Shack. Not far from here.' He paused. 'Want some company?'

'That'd be great.'

He disappeared and came back in a fresh shirt, cleaned up in a lick-and-a-promise sort of way. I followed his open Jeep five or six blocks and a couple of turns to The Shack, appropriately named and not someplace I'd have gone into without a recommendation. The parking lot was packed, though, usually a good sign.

THIRTY-FOUR

'The food's better than the décor,' he promised with a grin as we stepped inside, immediately surrounded with noise. He said something I couldn't hear.

'What?' I yelled. 'Sorry. I can't hear.'

Captain Dave leaned close to my ear. 'There's a booth in the back. I'll block. You follow.' Dave spoke to a dozen or more people on the way, but we made it to the corner booth at the far end of the narrow room. He grinned. 'Offensive line. Boston College. Don't let anybody tell you football's not a life skill.'

'If I didn't appreciate that before, I do now,' I answered, speaking loudly to be heard over the roar of laughter, conversation and music. 'You must be a regular.'

He nodded. 'The fish is fresh. I know who they buy it from. The rest of the food is good, too. And Jack, the owner, has been known to stand a meal or two when times are lean.' He grinned apologetically. 'And no tourists.'

I nodded. I'd lived through my share of Fan Fairs and CMA Weeks in Nashville. I understood.

I pulled a menu, laminated in plastic, from behind a paper towel holder. 'What do you recommend?'

'Grouper's been running good, but we'll ask.'

A waitress appeared then, no nonsense in jeans and a red T-shirt that said The Shack. 'Hey, Dave, what'll it be?'

'What's the best thing in the kitchen?'

'Grouper's good, but the flounder's great.'

'Bring me flounder. Pan-fried.'

'Sweet tea, baked potato, blue cheese?' He nodded, and the waitress turned to me.

'I'll have the same.'

She nodded and was gone.

'You order like a Southerner,' I said. 'How long have you been here?'

'Ten years, more or less. Long enough when I go back up
east to visit, I don't sound like my family anymore.'

I smiled, thinking how very Boston he sounded to me.

Two big glasses of iced tea materialized, sweating in the
humid air. The restaurant was air conditioned, and fans turned,
hanging from the high ceiling, but the crush of bodies and
Miami summer kept the room from being cool.

Captain Dave's face turned solemn. 'I'm sorry about your
friend.'

'Thank you,' I said. Neither of us spoke for a minute. I
wondered what he meant. Fly's death? Or the implications of
a hidden briefcase full of cash? Dave looked out the window
to the Miami twilight. Then I asked the question I'd been
wanting to ask since the first time I'd called him. 'Did it make
sense to you?' He looked up. 'Did it make sense that he'd sail
right into that storm? Was he being reckless?'

He took a deep breath and sighed. 'Hindsight.' He shrugged.
'We have storms every day somewhere. Maybe not literally
every day, but this time of year, you don't have many days
without a chance of storms. If he'd been more experienced,
could he have outrun it? Maybe. It did change direction.' Dave
looked up, hesitated. 'If he hadn't been hit by the boom,
apparently knocked overboard, he'd probably have been fine.
The boat only had minor damage.' He shook his head. 'It's
not Disney World. Accidents happen. Even, sometimes, when
you're reasonably well prepared and careful.' He stopped, as
if he were through, then spoke again. 'He didn't strike me
as a careless man.'

The waitress reappeared with salads, real mixed greens,
tomatoes, cheese, bacon. Fresh. 'Blue cheese. Anything else
right now? OK.' She vanished into the crowd before we had
time to answer.

Dave went on, pouring salad dressing from the plastic cup
onto his salad, spearing greens. 'It's hard for families to accept
death at sea, even families who've lived off the sea for gener-
ations. I guess it's as long as there's no body, you can hope.
My grandfather was a fisherman. Out of Gloucester. I've seen
it all my life. The truth is, the sea's a dangerous place to be.
Men go out to sea every day. And every man who comes back

is lucky. And most know it.' He took another deep breath, and the grin was back. 'But don't tell my insurance agent I said that.'

With unspoken agreement, we left the subject of Fly. The flounder was pan-fried with garlic, lemon and just the right seasonings. A small cup on the side held a sauce with tiny shrimp. Even the potato was good and didn't seem to have been sitting for hours in a warmer.

Dave told me fish stories, a few of which might have been true, and I began to envy him as I laughed with him. How often do you meet someone who really is living out his dream? And enjoying every minute of it. By the time we were ready to think about dessert, the waitress had time to do more than bring us food and drink.

'You guys want some dessert? We got homemade pecan and chocolate pie tonight.'

'Campbell?' Dave waited for me to decide.

'No, I don't think so. But I would like some coffee.'

'Me, too, Laney,' Dave said to the waitress. 'Campbell, this is Laney Simon. Laney, Campbell Hale. Campbell knew Franklin Young.'

'The guy who drowned? Oh, I'm sorry, hon. He came in here once in a while. Seemed like a nice guy. He was in a couple of times recently. In fact . . .' A customer at the next table caught her attention. 'You need a refill? OK, be right there.' She turned back to us. 'I'll be right back with your coffee.'

In seconds, she was pouring refills of coffee at the next table and setting hot cups in front of us. 'Yeah,' she went on as if there had been no interruption, 'I thought I saw him the night of the storm, but I must've been confused. This place is enough to keep me confused. Maybe it was the night before. I'm pretty sure he'd been in before he went out. He had a condo near here, didn't he? And then I saw his picture on TV.' She shook her head. 'Hard to believe.'

An hour and a half later we were on the sidewalk in what passed for the cool of a Miami summer evening, stuffed, exchanging cards and 'if you're ever in . . .'. I promised to show him the best barbecue in Middle Tennessee. He walked me to the rental car and raised his hand as I pulled out into the Miami night.

THIRTY-FIVE

B ack in the condominium parking lot, I debated what to take inside. The laptop, legal pad with the long number, the briefcase we'd found behind the bulkhead. I'd already gone through the duffel and the box, so I decided I'd leave them in the car. I left the camera there, too. I couldn't open the briefcase unless I found a key – and I probably shouldn't then. My job was to take it back to Nashville, and the less I knew, the better.

But if I did find a key inside or in any of Fly's stuff, I'd open that briefcase. And I wanted to take a look at what was on that laptop.

There could be a lot of reasons, good reasons, why Fly would have had cash with him. He hadn't been leaving the country with it. It wasn't on the chartered boat. He'd left it in the boatyard, secure in the boat he intended to leave here for several weeks. Maybe he always kept cash with him when he traveled. I was beginning to feel nervous, standing here in a dark parking lot, holding what might be a lot of money, even if no one else knew that.

No one else except Captain Dave. And my note writer. I'd forgotten about him. I didn't know who he was, but he didn't have any trouble with locked doors. I didn't think I wanted to spend the night waiting for him. I didn't have to stay here. I could get a room. Yeah. I'd look around in there one more time, maybe get the night manager to come up with me, then get my stuff and call for a hotel reservation.

I put a strap over each shoulder and shut the trunk. And suddenly I was afraid. I started toward the light, toward the front door, in a hurry now.

I was in shadows, blocked from the view of the door by a large palm and landscaping shrubs when I heard footsteps behind me. I held the laptop and briefcase close with my elbows and walked fast and purposefully, just like they always tell you to do in those self-defense seminars for women. It didn't work.

I heard the steps quicken, and in that instant something hit my back, shoving me to the ground, my face against the asphalt. The briefcase and laptop were jerked off my shoulders, and he was gone. I saw a dark shape, dark clothes, a baseball hat pulled low, as he melted into more shrubs at the edge of the lot.

The air had been knocked from my lungs, and I gasped, too shocked to scream if I'd been able. Another yard and I'd have been in a pool of light in full view of the door and the night manager inside. I stood and took inventory, trying hard not to throw up. My knees were scraped, but not much blood. My right shoulder hurt; my left elbow was bleeding. I was gulping air and starting to sob.

The laptop was gone. The briefcase was gone – with whatever was inside and any hope for answers. How was I going to explain this to Erika?

The manager saw me and rushed out. 'Ah, *Dios! Que pasa?* Are you OK? What happened?'

I shook my head, pointing, trying to explain, still gasping and trying to breathe. 'I . . . I . . . Call . . . the police. Please. I . . .'

'*Sí, sí.* I will call. Come inside.'

I went inside and waited, shivering and shaking, while he called the police. I tried to follow the exchange, but part was in Spanish, part in English with a lot of nodding and head shaking, and my head was beginning to hurt. He hung up and turned to me, apologetic.

'I am so sorry. A policeman will come, fill out a report, but nothing will happen. That's the way it is. You are not hurt badly; nothing will happen.' He seemed as distraught as I felt and outraged at the low priority my crime had. I wasn't surprised. I doubted if things would be much different in Nashville. But it wasn't as if what had been stolen could be replaced.

I was responsible to Erika and Marcella for Fly's things,

and now they were gone. Whatever answers might have been with them were gone, too. They'd have been better off with FedEx.

THIRTY-SIX

T he policeman who came to take my report was courteous and sympathetic, but he didn't offer much hope. I couldn't offer much information on the contents. I felt sure I could get the laptop serial number from Marcella the next day, but I couldn't tell him what was in the briefcase. I didn't know. And what I was afraid was in the case – cash – wouldn't sound good to the people who were already concerned about Fly's business affairs.

The night manager had waited supportively in the condominium with me for the officer to come, but he couldn't help either. He hadn't seen what happened. I wasn't sure I wanted to tell the policeman about the note I'd found, especially now that the briefcase was gone.

When the nice policeman and the solicitous manager were finally gone and I'd washed all my cuts and scrapes and decided nothing was seriously hurt, when I had a chance to sit down with some ice on the bruises, then I could finally think.

Had this been a random street crime? Wasn't that what Sam had called Charles Patton's murder? Was I just in the wrong place at the wrong time, a vulnerable looking woman, alone in a dark spot in the parking lot of an upscale condominium, carrying stuff that might be worth the cost of a fix? Was it just my luck that a purse-snatcher happened to get the personal things Fly Young had taken with him almost to his grave? Or had the person who'd left the note waited to claim what he wanted?

Captain Dave knew what I had, but if he'd wanted to take Fly's things, he could have before now. No one had known what Fly had with him. Of course, Captain Dave hadn't known about the hidden briefcase until we found it together.

He didn't know any more than I did about what was inside, but he knew as much. He had felt those rectangular shapes that might have been bundles of cash. But he'd been with me through supper. When could he have set up a mugging?

Was I trying to manufacture a conspiracy? I tried to reconstruct the mugging in my mind. It had happened so fast. And when I looked up I couldn't see much. Medium build. Too small to have been Captain Dave. I had an impression that he, yes, a man, was a little taller than me. That's about the only thing I was sure of. But there was something . . . Something about him had felt familiar. Unless it was my paranoia. Was it a scent? A shampoo or soap or aftershave I knew? I couldn't pull it out.

It was too late to call Nashville, and there was nothing they could do anyway. I checked the locks on all the doors. The manager had ordered one security guard to stay in the hallway outside my door and another to stay within sight of the balcony. I started to get a Coke but decided I didn't need the caffeine. I poured a glass of juice, swallowed a couple of aspirin and sat in a corner of the couch in the beautiful living room, holding ice to my face until I fell asleep. I dreamed of storms and dark, angry seas. Fly was there, urging me to put on a life vest. And I would have, too, if I could have found one.

THIRTY-SEVEN

I woke up early the next morning, stiff from sleeping on the couch, and couldn't go back to sleep. I walked on the beach, hoping for some clarity. Had Fly made some deal with someone here in Miami, someone who had reason to expect something valuable, cash or whatever, was still on the boat Fly had sailed from Nashville? A bag full of cash on a boat? I couldn't believe Fly was dealing drugs.

Who could have left the note for me? How had he/she gotten into the condominium? I knew Erika was using me, but she was in Nashville making a video to show women how easy it

was to look like her – except, of course, that they'd also
have to buy the next video and the next book. Had she sent
someone to grab what I found? But if she knew something was
hidden, why not tell me in the first place to look for it. An
hour on the beach didn't give me any answers, so I gave up.

I made coffee and waited until I thought Marcella would
be in the office. I called. She was disappointed, but what could
she say? 'You're not hurt, though?' she asked.

I assured her I was OK.

'I wish we knew what was in there, in the bag as well as
Fly's laptop,' Marcella said. 'It may be just as well. Today an
auditor asked if he had one. Things are heating up. We've
been told not to shred anything, not even routine stuff.'

'I really feel bad about this, but there was nothing I could
do. And the police don't think anything will turn up. I'll get
them to send copies of their report.'

'No, no. I know,' Marcella said. 'Don't feel bad. Talk about
bad luck. Look, you were doing us a favor. You know you're
welcome to stay there a few days, rest up.'

Was she kidding? Rest? In this place? 'I need to get back.'
I paused. 'I'm not looking forward to telling Erika. She really
is in Nashville, right?'

'Yeah, she came by the office late yesterday afternoon.
Why?'

Silly to suspect her of having me mugged. 'I'm afraid she
may not be as understanding.'

'No. I'll tell her.' Marcella laughed. 'I'll send her an email.
Maybe she'll take some of it out on somebody else before
you get back to town.'

'Great. Now I can feel good about ruining their day, too.'

My next call was to Captain Dave. 'Would I be paranoid
to wonder if somebody saw us and followed me?'

'Probably,' he said. 'José was the only one in the yard when
we were on the boat. He's worked with me for years. And he
was gone before we left the yard. As a general rule I don't
believe in coincidence, but I don't see it. Unless it was whoever
told you to look for it.'

'Yeah, whoever that was. And now I'm not likely to find
out.'

'I'm sorry.' Then he tried for a lighter tone. 'If you'd asked me back to your place, this would never have happened, you know.'

'Does that approach work for you? "I'm better than a mugging"?' I could finally laugh about the whole thing.

'Sometimes. Next time you're in Miami you should keep that in mind.'

'Next time.'

So much for my one-day beach vacation. I did go to the pool. I swam ten laps, then turned on my back and floated. I tried not to think. Nothing was making sense anyway. I just floated, rising and falling with the water as other people swam, jumped and played. The water simmered in the sun, almost too hot to be refreshing. I closed my eyes, trying to escape muggers and unpleasant wives and questions that didn't have answers. I smelled cocoa butter, the smell of summer, then, later, something sweet, fruity, a spilled drink maybe.

I heard a woman say, 'She's not moving. You think she's OK?'

I moved my hands, finning slightly so they'd know I hadn't drowned.

I'd been doing what everyone asked me to do. Fly, Marcella, Erika, my mysterious note writer. Just tell me what you need, I'll do it. And I had no idea what was going on. Had Fly been embezzling money from his company and from his wife's? Had he been planning to leave the country? Who would have stopped him? All he had to do was call me, say, Campbell, I need a ticket to Grand Cayman, to Freeport, Nassau, to Bermuda, anywhere tropical with beaches and fruity drinks and, it goes without saying, banks with numbered accounts and bankers who don't feel they have to tell the US government everybody's business. And I'd have said, aisle or window? Of course, if he really was skipping the country with investors' money – and Erika's – somebody would have followed pretty soon.

It would be a lot easier to enjoy your margaritas without looking over your shoulder if nobody was looking for you.

Was Fly Young alive?

Had he staged his own death?

Had Fly figured a way to start his life over after all?

A bad storm, but not an unsurviveable storm. Not with a life raft, water, an extra life vest. A little blood on the boom to buy time. A little Polysporin to heal the cut. A new set of identification documents, a driver's license, a passport, a little cash stashed away. Not for a man who knew what he was doing. And was prepared.

THIRTY-EIGHT

I was back in Nashville by six. I called Erika from the car on the way home, but an assistant told me she was in a meeting. I called Marcella's number and found her still at work.

'Yeah, we're all working late. Erika's here. She's screaming at George and Al and the lawyers. She wants them to buy her out.'

'Buy her out?'

'Yeah, the way the company's set up, if a partner dies, the remaining partners have first option on his share. She wants the money, and she wants it now. And now's not a good time.'

'I guess not.'

'There's no money to buy her out. Not that kind of cash anyway. And there's no way the auditors and lawyers are going to allow that right now. Everything's frozen except current operating funds.'

'So what's going to happen?'

'I think Erika's not going to get what she wants for once.'

'That's going to put her in a good mood when I talk to her.'

'Yeah, well, I think it's going to be a long, long time before Erika's in a good mood.'

That wasn't good news, but it was a reprieve. At least I didn't have to talk to her immediately. Instead I could go pick up Sandy, my cat who would have missed me and be glad to lick my ankle.

I called MaryNell.

'Sure,' she said. 'You can eat supper with us, too. I want to hear everything.'

I stopped by Walgreen's to make prints from the photos on my phone and my camera. I have a secret fear that Walgreen's is part of a plot to take over the world. It started slowly, one here, one there, open twenty-four hours. Then another corner, another. Convenient, handy. Now there's one on most every corner in town. How many drug stores do we need?

At MaryNell's, I rang the bell, and Melissa opened the door. 'Hey,' she said. 'Heard you were mugged. Cool! You OK?'

'Yeah, I'm fine.' I showed her the scabs on my elbow. 'How's Sandy?'

'Fine. I've been teaching him tricks.'

I followed her to the kitchen.

'Hey, you're back! In one piece.' The edge in MaryNell's voice told me that after supper I'd have to listen to another lecture on putting myself in danger.

'Hi. Hi, Julie.'

'Hey, Miss Hale.'

'Sit down. I'll get you a glass of tea.' MaryNell mothered.

'Where's Sandy?'

'Around somewhere. Probably with Fluffy.'

Fluffy. What kind of name is that for a cat? I didn't say that out loud, of course. 'Where's Roger?'

'He's at church.'

'Mission meeting or something?'

MaryNell rolled her eyes. 'Summer league church basketball. Record number of torn ACLs this season.'

I laughed. 'Good, clean fun.'

'Yeah. He won't admit it's harder every year. None of them will. It's just these young kids, you know. They play rougher. The game's changed.'

'Speaking of young kids, we're off.' Melissa and Julie had finished eating. They carried dishes to the sink.

'OK. Let me know or tell your dad if you're going anywhere afterwards.'

'Bye, Campbell,' Melissa said.

Julie echoed. 'Bye, Miss Hale. Thanks for supper, Mrs McLean.'

And they were gone.

MaryNell sat down across from me. She sliced a generous piece of quiche and put it on the plate she had set out for me. 'Have some fruit.' She offered the bowl of grapes and strawberries.

'Thanks.'

'Now. I want the whole story.'

I told her everything I knew.

She interrupted with questions about Captain Dave. 'O line at Boston College? I like that. I mean, defensive linemen can be, well, animals, but offensive linemen are teddy bears. Like Bruce Matthews, used to be with the Titans? Or Keydrick Vincent, with Pittsburgh. Everybody needs an offensive line.'

'I thought you were head cheerleader for the gun-totin' Sam Davis.'

'It never hurts to have a deep bench,' MaryNell said.

'One more football metaphor and I program your V-chip to block ESPN from your TV.'

'OK, OK, so what happened when you talked to Erika?'

'I haven't yet. I've left messages. I'll go by tomorrow and take the things I did get back with. I'm not looking forward to this. Want to go with me?'

'Ah, no,' she said decisively.

'OK. Now I know the limits of our friendship.'

'I kept your cat for you while you were out of town.'

'I only have the cat because you dumped it on me.'

'Yes, but now you love him.'

'Well, if you're not going to go with me to face Erika, I'll just take my cat and go home.'

MaryNell laughed. 'I'll find him. He's playing with Fluffy.'

I followed her through the dining room, into the great room, down the hall. We found them in Melissa's room on a table in front of the window pretending to be Egyptian sphinxes. Sandy gave me a look, and I knew not to embarrass him by talking to him, asking him if he'd missed me, using the word 'cute'. I lured him into his carrier and went home.

THIRTY-NINE

A t home I checked my messages. Nothing from Sam. One from Erika Young returning my earlier call. Putting that one off wouldn't help. I filled Sandy's water bowl, put out a little food; he'd already eaten at MaryNell's.

I called, and this time we connected.

'I'd like to bring you the things from the boats,' I told her.

'Of course. I have meetings early. Everything is upside down. Can you come at one?'

'One. Yes, I'll see you then. Can you give me directions?'

'Of course.' Erika told me how to find her house, west on Harding Place into Belle Meade, right on Lynwood, then a couple more turns. 'I'll be working around back, by the pool. I'm sending the staff away so I can get some things done. So come on around back. There's no handle on the front of the gate, but you can reach over it and open it from the inside.'

'OK.'

'I'll expect you at one, then.'

I might as well look through Fly's things, I thought, as long as I had them. I unpacked my own bag, started a load of laundry, and settled down with Sandy beside me and the duffle of things I'd collected from the *Manana* and Captain Dave's boat. There wasn't much. I went through the pockets of the few clothes, flipped through the pages of the Bible and the other books, not even knowing what I was looking for. I opened the CD and DVD cases, looking behind the liners. Nothing. I flipped through the yellow pad. There, on the last page, was that number I'd seen earlier. Nothing else on the page, and it was written on the last page of an almost empty pad. You wouldn't see it unless you were looking, unless you either knew it was there or were searching. 010914 664 3298723 9845. I had no idea what it was. It might be nothing, a phone number with extension, or it might be a password, although it seemed too long for that. I didn't know, but I copied it.

I repacked the duffel. Not much there. Maybe Fly's children or his mother would be glad to have his Bible. I put it all by the front door and followed Sandy's example. I went to bed.

FORTY

The next morning I left for work before seven. I promised Sandy I'd be home early and play with him then. I picked up my Bahamas pictures at Walgreen's and debated whether I had time for a ham waffle at Pancake Pantry, thin chunks of ham cooked right into the waffle, but I knew there'd be a list of calls waiting for me to return. I settled for coffee.

I was right. There was a list but, thank goodness, no crisis. I worked steadily until twelve fifteen and left, drove through Burger King for a Whopper Jr and Coke and ate lunch on my way to Fly and Erika Young's Belle Meade mansion. That's how the newspapers always describe homes in Belle Meade; they're all Belle Meade mansions. When I pulled up in front of the Young house, I understood why. I parked in a gravel area off the circular drive and took a deep breath. Why, *why* had I agreed to bring this stuff back? And why couldn't I have just dropped it off at the HealthwaRx office? And why did I think it was a good idea to eat a hamburger on the way over here? Please, God, don't let me throw up all over her perfect driveway.

I looked for the gate. I could see the white, solid board fence that protected the back lawn. It was at least six-feet high. And it seemed to be growing as I watched. OK. Deep breath. I had to get this through-the-looking-glass feeling under control. To the left the fence seemed to stretch in an unbroken line. I walked toward the right. Just around the corner of the house, I saw the gate, solid boards painted white like the fence. An arbor arched over it supporting miniature coral roses. The gate, I saw, wasn't as high as the rest of the fence.

Up close, I saw that I could stand on my toes and reach over the top. I felt and found the latch. If only I could see how it worked. I stretched, fumbled, moving whatever seemed to move. There! Something gave, and the gate moved toward me. I stepped back and opened it. I smoothed my long linen shirt, tried to look professional, not like I'd just been breaking and entering. It was hot, and I was feeling less and less fresh every minute. I picked up the duffel and box and stepped onto grass like I'd never seen off a country club green. Flagstones marked a path toward the terrace and the pool.

'Erika? Mrs Young?' I called out because I didn't want to take her by surprise. No answer. I circled the side of the house and saw the landscaped pool, long, cool and blue, with a pool house beyond. I called again. 'Mrs Young!' I heard birds, a dog in the distance, nothing else.

At the back of the house, in the shade on the terrace between the house and the pool, there were lounge chairs and an outdoor table with chairs shaded by a blue sailcloth umbrella. An open laptop hummed quietly on the table. Papers fluttered in the slight breeze, too slight to relieve the oppressive heat.

If I lived here, I'd be in the pool today. Nothing else made sense outside on a day like today. I moved closer. Rocks and plants surrounded the pool so that water seemed to flow from a small woodland stream into it. Ferns fluttered. Water gurgled, and the filter hummed. I waved away a bee.

Maybe Erika had gone inside. I could sit at the table and wait.

I walked onto the terrace, looked back at the artificially natural pool and saw a woman floating. Long blonde hair. Erika was in the pool after all, and I couldn't blame her.

But something was wrong. She wasn't wearing a swimsuit but khaki shorts and a pink knit shirt. And she was floating, but face down, and nothing moved except her hair, eddying around her.

'Erika!' I screamed. 'Help! Erika!' I ran the few steps and splashed into the shallow, near end of the pool.

I reached her and rolled her over to see those blue eyes staring, open and lifeless. I screamed. Then I wanted to get away. I took a deep breath. What should I do first? I scrambled

out of the pool, my clothes dripping, and looked around. A
phone was on the table. I punched 911.

'Metropolitan Police. What is your emergency?'

'There's been an accident! There's a woman in the pool!'

The calm voice, a woman's, replied, 'Is she breathing,
ma'am?'

'I don't think so.'

'Do you know how long she's been in the water?'

'No! No! I just got here!'

'Can you confirm your address, ma'am?'

'Uh, uh . . .' I tried to think, then recited the Youngs' street
address. 'Belle Meade.' I didn't know the zip code.

'OK, and what's your name?'

'There's a woman in the pool! I think she's dead!'

'I've got somebody on the way. Now, what's your name?'

'I'm Campbell Hale, but it's not my house.'

'OK, Campbell. Why do you think the woman's dead?'

'She's not moving! Her eyes are open, and I couldn't feel
a pulse! Should I try to do CPR?'

'Are you trained in CPR, Campbell?'

I could hardly speak, and I couldn't think. I'd had a CPR
class ages ago, but I'd never tried it on anything except a
dummy torso.

'I think so. I mean, I had a course once. I think I can
do it.' The voice was working. I was a long way from calm,
but I was beginning to come back from the edge of panic.
'Can you tell me what to do?'

'Sure. We'll do this together, Campbell. First you need to
get her face out of the water. Can you do that?'

In the distance I could hear the first sirens. Thank you, God.

'I think so.'

I splashed back into the pool and over to Erika. I pulled her
over to the side of the pool, to the steps where I could get
her upper body out of the water and support her head.

'Campbell, you there?'

'Yeah, yeah, I'm here. OK. I've got her head out of the
water.'

'Can you get her out of the pool?'

'I can try. The gate is latched. Should I go unlock it?'

'No, you stay with the woman. Lean her head back. Make sure there's nothing in her mouth.'

Step by step, as I balanced the phone against my shoulder, she walked me through the CPR procedure, reminding me of the lessons I hadn't used in years. Breathe. Two. Three. Press. Press. It was hopeless. What was that song you were supposed to use to time the presses? I could tell it was hopeless, but I kept going. And kept going.

Then policemen were coming through the gate, the lighter blue Belle Meade uniform instead of Metro's dark navy. I was so relieved to see them. Finally. Somebody to take charge, to handle this. I started to cry.

They saw Erika and started to run toward her. Then things happened so fast, it was all a blur. I could hear more sirens, then white-shirted emergency medical personnel were coming through the gate. I was pushed aside and stood there dripping and crying. Then a young Metro officer was standing in front of me with a metal clipboard.

'Ma'am? Ma'am? Can you answer a few questions for me?'

I tried to focus on his face and nodded. My name. I could answer that, at least. I answered all his questions, my address and so on, stuttering and shaking, until he got to the ones that really mattered. What was I doing here, and what had I seen when I got here?

'Are you OK, ma'am? Why don't we step out to my car and sit down?'

The officer led me through the gate, and I saw television trucks with dish antennas. He held his clipboard up to shield my face. I saw other officers unrolling yellow police tape to mark a boundary. The officer opened a passenger side door for me and circled to the driver's side, leaving my door open. At least he hadn't caged me in the back.

'I don't want to make you too cold. I know it's hot, but your clothes are wet, and you've had a shock. When you get ready I'll turn some air conditioning on.'

I nodded and realized I was shivering.

'Now,' he continued, 'why don't you tell me what happened?'

I told him, step by step, what had happened from the time I'd gotten out of my car in Erika's drive. Told him why

I was there, about talking to her earlier. Occasionally, he stopped me to clarify something or ask me to repeat something. He nodded as he wrote, flipping over to the next page, then back. With another part of my brain I still heard sirens, the crackling of police radios, urgent conversations and the calm voices of implacable authority keeping neighbors and reporters at bay. Clouds were gathering.

The paramedics hurried by, pushing Erika strapped on a stretcher to the ambulance. More sirens and lights as they sped away.

'Campbell?'

'Sam?' He always seemed to show up at the worst times of my life. I was so glad to see him. I stood up and reached to hug him. He took my arms, his hands just above my elbows.

'Are you OK?' He looked into my eyes but held me away from him. He was wearing the cop face. Of course, I realized, he was working. He didn't need to be seen hugging me in front of the entire police force and media. That's OK; I was still relieved that he was there.

'I'm OK, but it was horrible! Oh, Sam! I didn't know what to do.'

'Stay here with Jack,' he said.

'Sam! She didn't fall into the pool, did she?'

'Stay here. I'll be back.'

I sat back in the car, and the rain that had been threatening fell with a vengeance. Lightning struck over and over again, close. I sat in the patrol car with the officer Sam had called Jack and watched the water pour down the windows. It poured down the front of the huge white house, down the huge columns, down the well-groomed trees. At least it sent the neighbors home and the reporters to huddle in their vans. It rained for half an hour or so, but it seemed like days. Or an instant. It stopped and moved east. I could see the clouds and lightning moving, probably over my house next.

The sun began filtering through the clouds and moisture hanging in the air. A steam bath. Policemen, uniformed and not, but all soaked and dripping, began filtering from behind the house. Finally Sam came back to the car.

'Thanks, Jack.'

'Yes, sir.'

'Campbell, we're gonna need you to come downtown, go over this with us. I'll ride in with you.'

I nodded. Jack handed forms to Sam, and Sam walked with me to the Spider, forlornly cheerful now in a sea of blue and whites and dark sedans.

Sam wasn't talking much. 'You want me to drive?' he asked.

I looked down and saw that my hands were still shaking. 'Yeah. Yeah. Thanks.'

Sam started the car and pulled away down the street with the beautiful houses, sparkling with raindrops, the green of the lawns and the color of every flower intensified.

'I think I want a Coke,' I said. 'You want one?'

Sam nodded. 'I guess.'

He pulled into the first fast food drive-through we came to and ordered two Cokes. I was hoping it would settle my stomach. Wash away the taste of chlorine. And death. I took a long drink. I wasn't sure it helped.

Sam sighed. 'Why don't you tell me what happened? And this time, please, don't leave anything out.' I heard a little sarcasm there.

'Where do you want me to start? She told me to come here—'

Sam interrupted. 'Why don't you just start with Miami?'

So I did.

Sam shook his head a lot. He stopped me when I got to the mugging and asked me to repeat a lot of it. As much as I could see glancing sideways at him while he drove, he seemed to be clenching his jaw a lot.

'Tell me again,' he said, 'exactly what she said to you on the phone last night.'

I told him.

'Did she say who she was meeting with?'

'No. She just said she would be working at home, outside by the pool.'

'Did you see anyone when you drove up, any car driving away?'

I shrugged. 'No. I don't think so. Not that I noticed. I was too nervous about talking to her to think about anything else.'

He sighed again. 'Between you, the paramedics and the rain, there's not much left of the scene.'

My eyes filled, but I was determined he wouldn't make me cry. 'What was I supposed to do?'

He shook his head. 'No, you did the right thing. But since you started CPR, they kept on. It's policy. Once CPR is started, you don't make the call in the field. The paramedics keep it up until they get to the hospital. You'd feel a lot worse if you hadn't tried. And I can't hold you responsible for the rain.' He sounded tired, but, hey, there was a lot of that going around.

FORTY-ONE

Downtown, in Sam's office in the Criminal Justice Center, I went through the whole thing again with a tape recorder running. And then again. And again. Every now and then, he'd add a question or ask one a little differently. By the time I was through it was too late to go back to work. Sam walked me to my car, waving off reporters. He was protecting me, but he wasn't . . . I don't know; he was a policeman. The policeman was escorting the material witness. It didn't have anything to do with friends.

At home I took aspirin and lay on the couch drinking water. I'd spent so long in the heat and sun at Erika's that I had a headache and felt dehydrated. Sandy sat on the floor beside me and occasionally made soft, comforting kitten noises. Finally, I turned on the ten o'clock news. There was the house, policemen standing around. I remembered seeing some of them. There was Sam. There I was, my hand up to my face like every felon I've ever seen on TV, rushing to my car.

And then her fans.

'Dan, tonight dozens of women are keeping a vigil outside Erika Young's Belle Meade home.' Candles lit the night behind the television reporter. 'They're mourning the loss of the woman who showed them how to search for balance in their lives, and each one has a story.' She turned to a tearful woman standing beside her. 'This is Emily Foster. Emily, why are you here tonight?'

'Erika Young changed my life,' she said earnestly. She waved, including the women who crowded behind her. 'That's why we're all here. We want Erika's children to know how much she meant to us, that we're with them, and we won't rest until her murderer is behind bars where she belongs.'

She? Me?

'Dan, these women have pledged to maintain this vigil until this crime is solved.'

I fell asleep wishing I'd never gone to that reunion.

FORTY-TWO

By Monday morning I was sure of it. At five thirty, I got a call from Mark at the newspaper.

'Hey, Campbell, I'm sorry, but this didn't come from me, and I couldn't do anything to stop it.'

'Huh?' I wasn't awake.

'There's a story in the paper about you finding Erika Young's body . . . and about you and Franklin Young. There's a photo.'

'What are you talking about?'

'There's a photo of you and Franklin Young. Kissing.'

'What?!'

'Yeah. Recent photo.'

I tried to think, tried to get awake. 'Oh, Mark. He drove me home after the reunion dinner. It was nothing. He kissed me once, an old time's sake kind of thing. It was nothing!'

'Yeah, well, with the magic of photography it doesn't look like nothing.'

'How could this be? How could there be a picture of that?'

'Apparently, she was having him followed. Apparently things were a little out of balance with the Youngs. It says you were unavailable for comment. Did anybody from the paper call you last night?'

'I unplugged the phone and turned off my cell. I called my

mom and MaryNell and just unplugged every phone in the house until I went to bed.'

'Well, you might want to call your mother again.'

My call waiting beeped, and I looked at the caller ID display. 'Too late. She's on the other line.'

'Have a nice day. Seriously, I'm sorry. I don't know about the police, but you're going to look like a suspect in the media. Be prepared.'

'Thanks.'

Then I called Mom back.

'Campbell? What is this pic—'

'It's not what it looks like, Mom,' I interrupted. 'It was nothing. That night he brought me home from the reunion, he kissed me goodnight.'

'He was a married man, Campbell!'

'It wasn't an affair, Mom. It was one kiss between old friends.'

'Well, it doesn't look good. It doesn't look good at all.'

'I know, Mom. I'm sorry.'

I ran to the driveway for my paper, but after Mom, there was MaryNell. Barbara. Melinda. And reporters. Thank goodness for caller ID. I threw the paper down without looking. Thanks to Mark's wake-up call, I managed to get ready for work and out the door in time to get to work early. I was inside with the door locked when the first reporter showed up. Lee and the others slipped through and locked the door behind themselves, but we knew we couldn't do business that way.

I gathered up some work to take home and was just about to leave when Sam and three other plain-clothes police officers walked in.

'Hi, Sam,' I said. Lee, Anna and Martha spoke to him, too, greeting him like an old friend.

Sam, however, just nodded, quick and curt.

Anna's eyes got big, and Lee told a client he'd call him back and assumed his wait-for-the-fireworks grin.

'Ms Hale?' A detective I'd seen yesterday spoke first.

'Yes.'

'We'd like you to come downtown with us. We've got a few questions to go over.'

'You know I was there all afternoon yesterday. What else is there?'

Sam was carefully examining the neutral tweed commercial carpet he was standing on.

'We're still trying to put everything together,' the officer said. 'We'd appreciate your helping us out.'

The attitude in the room didn't match the folksy, we're-all-in-this-together words.

'Sam?' I asked. 'What's this all about?'

Nobody said anything.

'Sam? Do I need to call a lawyer? Are you all arresting me?' I was beginning to get mad now. They could at least tell me what was going on. And Sam. He could at least speak to me.

'No, ma'am. We're just trying to get as much information as we can to make sense of all this. I'm Paul Green. We don't want to do anything official. We just need a little more of your time.'

I shrugged. 'OK.' I turned to Lee, who was enjoying all this way too much. 'Just take messages for me. I'll call you later. I'll go ahead and take this stuff with me and go on home from there.'

Lee nodded.

Anna said, 'Do you want me to call anybody? Your mom? MaryNell?'

I smiled. 'No. Thanks, though. At least, not yet. I'll let you know if I need bail.' My attempt to lighten the situation fell flat.

'Sam and I'll ride with you, if that's OK,' Detective Green said. 'Can I carry some of that for you?'

I looked at him and shrugged. 'Sure.' I tried to remind myself that he worked for me, that he was here to serve and protect me. It didn't work, but he could at least carry my files. 'Yeah, take these.' I handed him an eight-inch stack.

Sam held the door without meeting my eyes.

'Do you mind if I pick up a paper? At least I'd like to see what my mother's calling about.'

Paul Green looked at Sam. Sam shrugged. I stopped at a machine, dropped in some change and picked up a *Tennessean*.

I walked tall, trying for nonchalant and confident, as we headed for my car, Sam and Detective Green trailing. Sam still hadn't spoken a word.

I waited for Detective Green's reaction when we reached the Spider. I'd had three in this car before, but not three who believed the seat belt law applied to them.

Green sighed. 'Yeah, OK. I'll take my car. Sam, you ride with her.'

I opened the door, took my stack of papers and unlocked the passenger side for Sam.

'What about the other two?'

Sam didn't answer.

'What about the other two goons?' I was mad now.

Muscles moved in Sam's jaw. 'The other two *detectives* are none of your business.'

I glared at him and picked up my cell phone. 'Anna, hi. Yeah, so far. Look, are those other two police goons still there? . . . OK. If they touch anything, call me. And if you don't get me on the second ring, call . . . oh, call Doug. Yeah. Probably not, but at least he'll know what to do. It seems we're living in a police state. OK. Thanks. I'll call you later.'

Doug Elliott was my attorney and used to be one of my best friends. I used to hope he'd be more than that. But circumstances had made that unlikely, and we hadn't even talked to each other in months. I knew his character, though. I hadn't needed any legal services lately, but, even if he couldn't bring himself to speak to me, he'd help. He'd tell Anna what to do and find me a good lawyer with the right specialty.

'Are you going to tell me what's going on?' I asked.

'I was hoping maybe you'd tell me.'

'What are you talking about?'

Sam exploded. '"She's telling the truth," I tell them. "She might have screwed up the crime scene, but she didn't kill the woman. What motive would she have? She's not in love with the husband, I say. She's . . . she's dating me." I'm sticking my neck out. Then this morning we all read the paper.'

I hit the brake, stalled the car and barely avoided being hit by the car behind me. The driver swerved around me, leaning on his horn and gesturing impolitely at the same time. Multi-tasking.

I restarted the car and pulled into a parking lot. I was mad and scared and embarrassed and hurt and who knows what else. I grabbed the paper. There was the picture of Fly kissing me on my parents' back porch. My mom would be upset that she hadn't cleaned up the porch. My dad would just be upset.

The article quoted 'sources close to Franklin Young' as saying that a 'long-time romance' between Fly and me had been 'rekindled' at a high school reunion, that I had 'rushed to Miami' to 'the scene of search and rescue attempts', that I had stayed in 'Franklin Young's hideaway condominium' there. There were suggestions of 'hostility' between Erika and me. Sources in Florida and Nashville said I had taken things from two boats that I had not returned to Young's family and associates.

I turned to Sam, outraged, my mouth open.

'Save it,' he said. 'Make your statement downtown. I shouldn't even be alone with you. You know, I don't even care that this makes me look bad, that now it looks like I'm either a fool or withholding critical information. I can't protect you. Anything I do to help you is gonna look like you need help, like you're guilty. Anywhere I look besides you is gonna look like I'm trying to cover something up.'

'Are you arresting me?'

'Not yet. You better start the car. If we don't show up by the time Green gets there, somebody's gonna be out looking for us.'

FORTY-THREE

My hands were shaking, and I was trying not to cry as I started the car, my foot slipping off the clutch once, and pulled back into traffic. I couldn't help it if he hadn't called me. I'd have told him about Miami if he had. And I only went because Fly's office – and Erika – asked me

to. Not that she could support my story now. The search had
already been called off. And I was mugged! I was glad now
I'd filed a police report in Miami.

'So suddenly you believe everything you read in the
newspaper,' I said.

Sam shook his head, not disagreeing so much as dismissing
me. Neither of us spoke the rest of the way downtown.

Downtown I found that you have to pay to park even if
they're trying to decide whether or not to arrest you for murder.
'Next time I make you bring me in your car,' I muttered to
Sam.

'Next time?' he asked incredulously. 'Next time?'

Then I told my story again – just the way I had told it the
day before over and over. Except that I hadn't mentioned
before that Fly had kissed me. Once. On my parents' steps.
And nothing else.

Before I'd finished it, Doug arrived. He insisted they let
him into the room, and, when he did push his way in, Sam
didn't like it much.

'Doug?' I didn't know what I had expected if Anna called
him, but this wasn't it.

'I'd like to talk with my client.'

There was a lot of eye-rolling, but Sam, his buddy
Paul Green, and the other three who had been in the room
reluctantly left us alone.

'Doug, what are you doing here? I mean, not that I'm
not . . .'

'You're a murder suspect. You don't need to be talking to
anybody without a lawyer. I'm not the one you need. You
need a criminal attorney. But Bobby Jefferson couldn't make
if for a couple of hours, and I knew you couldn't keep quiet
that long.'

'I think I'm grateful,' I said uncertainly. Some things
hadn't changed. Doug still knew how to make me feel
incompetent. 'But I'm not a murder suspect. They can't
really think I did it.'

'Campbell! Who was there with the body?'

'I called nine-one-one!'

'Who was there with the body, alone? Whose fingerprints

are on the gate, the gate that was latched from the inside, by the way, and probably on the table?'

'Yeah, but I explained . . .'

'Who was photographed kissing her husband?' That did it. I burst into tears. And I'm not pretty when I cry. And then I get mad at myself because I don't want to cry. Which makes me cry more. At least Doug still carries a handkerchief. Not that he'd ever want that one back. It might as well have been a disposable tissue.

'The thing is,' Doug continued when I slowed down, 'they don't have anybody else. Everything they have on you might be circumstantial, but you're all they've got. If Franklin Young were around, they'd look at him first, but he's already dead. You're convenient.'

'I didn't touch that woman. Well, I did touch her, but she was already dead and only to make sure she was dead and to try to give her CPR. What was I supposed to do?' I was indignant now.

'I don't think you killed anybody. But when they say anything you say can be used against you, they don't mean it might be used against you. They mean anything you say, anything, they *will* use it against you.'

'But Sam wouldn't . . .'

'Campbell.' Doug silenced me. He sounded like my tenth grade algebra teacher.

'OK, OK,' I said. 'I've already told them what happened. All I can do is tell them the same thing again.'

'When I tell you to stop, stop. Not another word. If you're in the middle of a sentence, don't finish it.'

I nodded.

The detectives trooped back in, and Sam kept up this new fascination of his with floors, studying the boring, neutral tile, refusing to meet my eyes.

I went back through the story one more time with Doug making notes this time.

The detectives interrupted me several times, questioning what I'd done, why I'd done it. Sam's buddy Paul held up the newspaper photograph of Fly kissing me.

'Wanna explain this, Ms Hale?'

I looked at Sam. He was tracing the boundaries of the tile with the toe of his shoe. We might have been on different planets. I took a deep breath. I explained and tried not to cry. It was Sam's attitude that hurt most of all. He didn't trust me. Paul spread the newspaper across the table in front of me.

My cell phone rang. The office number showed on the screen. 'Hello.'

'Campbell, another detective just showed up with a warrant to search your computer.'

I turned to Doug. 'They're at my office with a warrant to search my computer. What do I do? I mean, there's nothing there. I haven't done anything! But, I mean, I work from that computer. If they mess it up . . .'

Doug leaned close to my ear. 'If they've got a warrant, they can search it. Is it backed up?'

'Yeah, I back it up every night.'

He nodded. 'OK, we'll take a look at your backup later.'

My backups were locked in the safe. I turned back to the phone. 'Thanks for calling me, Lee. I guess just let them do it, but keep an eye on them. If they mess up that reservation software . . .' I left that hanging. I didn't want to think about how much trouble it would be if we couldn't interface with the airlines' reservation systems. I called Lee back to remind him where to find the technical support phone numbers.

I gritted my teeth and turned back to Detective Green. 'He kissed me. I wasn't happy about it, but it was a kiss between old friends. Not an affair.' I saw a couple of the detectives sneak looks at Sam. His face was rigid except for the muscle clenching in his jaw. I knew that face. It wasn't a good sign. I was hurt, really hurt, but I was beginning to get mad. I didn't deserve this from Sam. 'One time,' I said quietly.

Green raised his eyebrows in a cynical question.

'Look,' I said, 'somebody was having him followed. Do you have any other photographs?' I was losing patience, and it showed in the edge in my voice. 'If there was anything going on between us, you'd have more pictures. And you don't.'

'OK, guys.' Doug spoke up. 'Enough. My client's been through this several times. I think that's enough.'

Nobody moved.

Doug stood. 'Campbell. Gentlemen, have a nice day.'

I followed him out the door. Sam still hadn't looked at me. Doug didn't stop until we were outside in the heat.

'You gonna be OK to drive home?'

'Yeah, sure.' Except for my hands shaking, I thought. And this feeling in my stomach like I might throw up any second.

'OK.' Doug handed me a business card. 'Give him a call if you haven't heard from him by three this afternoon.'

I nodded.

'Make sure you make contact with him today. If somebody doesn't walk in and confess to these guys pretty soon, they'll have you back down here. Don't come alone. You got it? If you can't get Bobby, you call me. You call me later and tell me what's going on.'

I nodded again. It felt good to have Doug back on my side. I needed somebody on my side. I shuddered and tried not to cry. 'Want your handkerchief?' I held it up.

It was Doug's turn to shudder. He backed up. 'No. You keep it.'

'I'll wash it and get it back to you.'

Doug waved it off.

'Thanks, Doug.'

He shrugged. 'Least I could do. After . . .'

It was my turn to wave away . . . what? Guilt? Responsibility? I was already too close to tears to delve into the layers of history there. Another time. 'Well, thanks. I'll call this guy.'

He nodded.

I waved, and we headed in opposite directions to our cars. I drove home with a weight in the pit of my stomach like one too many burritos late at night.

FORTY-FOUR

By the time I turned into the shade of my driveway, I was trying to come up with a plan. Counting Fly, three people close to that company had died. I couldn't just sit back and wait for the police to give up investigating and arrest me. I couldn't depend on Sam's help. Sam didn't even act as if he knew me. It felt a little like junior high, as if he didn't want the other boys to know he liked me, so he ignored me. Unless, of course, he really didn't like me. It hurt the same way. But if I was honest, I had to admit he was in an awkward position. How much more awkward would it be if they arrested me? I'd heard stories about how they treat cops in jail. How do they treat cops' girlfriends? Or ex-girlfriends.

I unlocked the door and opened it carefully so Sandy couldn't slip out. It was too hot out here to chase him down or supervise his playtime outside. I closed the door quickly behind me.

'Sandy?' I called. I expected him to come running, tiny claws scampering over the hardwood floors. 'Sandy?' I started for the kitchen to check his water bowl. Then I saw him. Looking at me. Not moving. Not blinking. Expectant. He sat on the coffee table on top of the newspaper I hadn't had time to look at this morning. 'Hey, boy, at least you're glad to see me, aren't you?'

Not a word. No change of expression.

'Hey, Sandy.' I needed a friendly face. Maybe that's what MaryNell meant about having a cat. It was nice to come home to an accepting friend who wasn't making judgments, to chill, not have to explain myself. I walked over to rub Sandy's back, soft and furry. 'You still love me, don't you, buddy?'

Then I saw where he was pointing. He'd seen the picture of Fly and me in the paper. '*Et* you, Sandy?' He stared at me steadily. Waiting.

'Yes, I knew he was married, but no, nothing was going on. I don't care what it looks like.' Sandy didn't blink, didn't say a word. 'I've told you the truth. If you don't trust me, that's your problem.'

Sandy slapped the newspaper photograph hard, just once, with his tail, then rose and walked away, leaping lightly to the floor and leaving the room. OK. If that's the way he wanted it, he could clean his own litter box.

I changed to shorts and a T-shirt, put out fresh water and

food for Sandy to show I was the bigger person, then scrounged around in the refrigerator. Not much there. I'd been too busy finding bodies and confounding the police lately to make it to the grocery store. There was one tomato, homegrown. My neighbor Mrs Morgan had brought me some from her garden. There is nothing in this world like a fresh tomato, homegrown and ripe from the vine. It may be the best thing about summer. I pulled out the last two slices of bread, Hellmann's mayonnaise, and started fixing a tomato sandwich.

I had way too many unanswered questions, beginning with who had killed Erika Young? Who could have wanted her dead? Any one of millions of women who had found out the hard way that her weight loss/lifestyle plan wouldn't really make them look like Taylor Swift and change their lives. Possible, but not likely. Who would benefit from her death? Hard to know without seeing her will, but presumably Fly would have if he hadn't died first.

If he had died first.

If he weren't the helpful burglar in Miami. And the selective, vaguely familiar mugger.

I sliced the tomato and tried to concentrate on the facts I knew about Fly's disappearance. Blood on the boom. Blood on the ripped life vest. Ouch! Blood on the counter! I should have been concentrating on the knife in my hand. I ran water over the tiny cut and pulled the last paper towel off the roll to wrap it. Tiny, but a lot of blood.

The blood on the boom and the vest was identified as Fly's type, but had they done a DNA match? Probably not. Too expensive. And slower. They'd probably just matched blood types. But assume it really was Fly's blood. If he really wanted to disappear, he could have cut himself, put blood where he wanted it. Extreme maybe, but possible. He didn't have to make a big cut. The life raft hadn't been used, but what was to stop him from having bought an extra life raft, even one with a small motor. He could have come ashore anywhere along the south Florida coast.

I got a tea bag, wet it and pressed it against my finger to stop the bleeding.

Why would a man with everything want to disappear and

leave it all behind? Or all of it that wouldn't fit into a canvas briefcase with a lock?

I put a Band-Aid on my finger and finished putting my sandwich together. Mayonnaise, sliced tomatoes, salt and pepper. Mmmm. I don't care what gourmet stuff you import from where, you can't beat a homegrown tomato sandwich in the summer.

Maybe because he'd taken some of it with him?

Erika's cash. HealthwaRx's cash. HealthwaRx's shareholders' cash.

Could Fly have done that to his family, to his children?

Could Fly have killed Erika?

Tomato sandwiches are a little messy, though. They tend to drip tomato juice. I reached under the kitchen sink for a new roll of paper towels. Platitudes. On the paper towels, one platitude after another. 'A trouble shared is a trouble halved.' How did I wind up with those? I usually buy solid white. 'A true friend is the best possession.'

I didn't know about possessing friends, but I was beginning to wonder how to know a true one. Sam wouldn't speak to me, and Fly . . . Who knew what Fly had done, if he was dead or alive, if he was just using me and everyone else around him?

I finished my sandwich standing at the counter. No point in dripping all over the furniture. I put my dirty dishes and knife in the dishwasher and washed my hands. 'First impressions are the most lasting.' What was my first impression of the adult Fly Young? I was wary. Suspicious. But was that about him – or me?

FORTY-FIVE

First on my list of things to do was to call Marcella.

'Hi, Campbell, I'm not supposed to talk to you.'

'What do you mean?'

'We had a staff meeting this morning. No one is supposed to talk to you. I could get in trouble just for this.'

'Why?'

'Well . . . Erika, you know. I mean, I don't think you killed her. And if you did, folks around here would probably chip in for a medal, but they think it looks funny if any of us are talking to the chief suspect in a partner's wife's murder.'

'Marcella! I only got mixed up in this because you asked me to go to Miami! Now my picture's in the paper, and it sounds like someone in your office is saying things that aren't true.'

'I know, and I feel really bad about getting you involved in this.'

'How can I find out who she was meeting with Friday morning?' I asked. 'And what about Charles Patton? Does anyone know who he was with right before he was killed?'

'Oh, Campbell, I really can't say any more. My job here's a little shaky anyway with Franklin gone. I'm really sorry.'

'What about the partners? Could she have been meeting with them?'

'No, no. They were both out of the office all day. Legal meetings, I think. Neither one of them came in until after lunch. I've got to go. Sorry.'

And she hung up.

Neither Al Evanston nor George Madison had been in the office Friday morning. It should be easy enough to find out if they'd really been meeting with lawyers. Easy for the police. Except they thought they already had Erika's murderer. Me.

Marcella could have found out for me where their meetings were, who they were meeting with. If she were still talking to me.

I wandered around the house. I thought about going outside to do some gardening. Digging in the dirt always seemed to help me think. But it was too hot, too humid.

At least I could work. I pulled out my file on the basketball trip to Freeport. I had picked up the photographs from my trip on the way home. Prints and a CD. I grabbed the prints, sat on the couch and turned the offending newspaper face down. Flipping through the prints, I thought how much had changed since I'd taken them. I sorted photos from the two properties into separate stacks. That should give the coaching staff an impression of each. A third stack was more general, street scenes, the straw market, the harbor. I looked through them. I could have spent a few days there, let Fly Young's people run their own errands. Then I wouldn't be a murder suspect. No good deed goes unpunished. They should put that on a paper towel.

Something caught my eye in a photo from a downtown street. I'd snapped a picture of a row of businesses, interesting architecture, tropical colors, and the people on the street, tourists, natives, a uniformed guard at a bank entrance. A man's face, eyes wide and startled, was turned toward the camera. The eyes stood out in contrast to the heavy beard. Fly Young! Fly Young? Was it Fly, scruffy and bearded, and surprised to see me pointing a camera at him? I looked at the picture next to it, snapped seconds before. There was the man again, coming out of the bank with the uniformed guard.

I grabbed the CD and ran to my computer. My hands were shaking, so it took me three tries to get it in the slot. I scanned through the photos until I found the one I wanted. I hadn't messed with photography software much, but I knew I could blow up certain parts, enhance the focus a little.

I zoomed in on the man with the beard and enlarged him. If I'd known more about this, I could probably have taken off the beard. I held my hand up to block the beard from view, focused on the eyes.

It was Fly. I was sure of it. He was alive!

And that meant he was a fraud!

Was he a murderer, too?

I reached for the phone and punched in the first two numbers of Sam's cell number. Then I disconnected. Deep breath. OK. Maybe he was being a jerk, but he was still more likely to pay attention to me than anybody else was. I punched in his number.

'Sam Davis. Please leave a message at the beep.' Voicemail.

'Sam, this is Campbell. I've got something you need to see. Please.'

I looked back at the screen. Fly was looking right at me. He must have thought I'd seen him. I wondered if he was really after my camera when he grabbed the bags in Miami.

If I couldn't get hold of Sam, what could I do?

There was noise outside. I realized I'd been hearing it for a while, ignoring it, but it was louder. And I lived on a very quiet street.

I opened the door to look out.

'There she is! Murderer!'

'Homewrecker!'

'Adulterer!'

There must have been a hundred women out there! With signs! And babies. Little children carrying signs with sayings like 'Justice for Erika' and 'Balance Justice'. They all started screaming when they saw me and rushed toward the door. As I slammed the door closed, I saw the television cameras.

I shot the deadbolt across as the pounding started on the door. Little kids thought I was a slut! I could hear the yelling through the door.

'Murderer!'

'Get your life in balance!'

'Tramp!'

And through the windows. Now they were trampling my impatiens and trying to look in the windows. That was too much. I couldn't close the drapes; I didn't have any. I closed shutters over the windows that had them, lace sheers over others.

'You can't hide from justice!'

What happened to innocent until proven guilty?

I ran back to the phone and called the police.

'There's an angry mob of women and children in your yard?' The dispatcher sounded skeptical.

OK, I was having a hard time believing it, myself. 'Yes, a mob with signs and stuff! And they're ruining my impatiens. And yelling in my windows!'

'Why?'

'I . . . They think I . . .'

'Oh, I recognize your name now. You're Sam Davis' friend. You're the one that found that Balance woman's body.' She laughed. How professional was that? 'Oh, honey, I bet you got some mad b . . . women in your yard. OK, I'll get somebody out there. They not breakin' in, are they?'

'Not yet.'

She was still laughing. 'Hang on, honey, we'll get somebody right out there. You call right back if it gets worse.'

They were pounding on the windows now.

I called MaryNell.

'You've got what in your yard?'

I tried to explain again, but I wasn't sure she could hear me. She was laughing too hard.

'Well, dieters have a lot of unresolved anger,' she offered. 'Chocolate deficiency. You know how people feed raw meat to attack dogs? You could put out some chocolate. But I'd throw it. As far away from your door as you can.'

'I can't open my door to throw it! They'd be all over me in a second!'

'Do you want me to come over?'

'It's too dangerous. I've called the police.'

'Which channel?'

'What?'

'Which channel are the TV cameras from?'

I tried to think what I'd seen as I slammed the door shut. 'Four? Five, maybe? I'm not sure.'

'OK. Call me back if it gets worse or you want me to come over. I could park over at the Morgans' and sneak in the back.'

'I don't think so. They've got me surrounded.' I could hear sirens now. 'Hey, I think the police are almost here. I'll call you back.'

The sirens got louder, how sweet a sound, shutting out the voices of little kids calling me names.

Police cruisers stopped in the street, sirens off but blue lights still flashing. 'Ladies! Ladies! Let's settle down.' I could see the police officers calming the crowd, gently moving them back from my house to the edge of the yard. I stood at the side of a window, trying to hide from view as I watched. The women began to march with more order but no less anger.

One police officer broke from the others and approached the door. He knocked. 'Ms Hale? Ms Hale?'

I opened it an inch and a half. 'Yes? Thanks for coming so fast. It was getting a little scary.'

He laughed. 'Yep. We've got us a situation out here. You OK?'

'Yeah. You want to come in?'

'Not if you're all right. We'll just hang around here for a little while.'

FORTY-SIX

Over his shoulder I could see a new arrival. MaryNell in a Lifestyle Balance T-shirt and carrying two large baskets. She walked purposefully to the middle of the long oval the women made as they marched at the edge of my yard. She pulled a bottle out of one basket and offered it to a woman wearing a baby in a back carrier and holding a sign that read 'Mothers for the Death Penalty'. MaryNell had brought refreshments. She started handing out bottles of water to the women marching in ninety-eight-degree heat. She offered the other basket, and several women reached inside. Candy bars. She'd brought candy bars.

'Looks like that's distracting them,' the policeman said.

'That's my best friend.'

'Really? And she's picketing you? Maybe you ought to think about gettin' out, meetin' new people.'

We watched as MaryNell handed both baskets over to marchers. She stood there a few more minutes, nodding forcefully, her hands on her hips. She raised a fist, then turned and started toward the door. As she reached the porch, she crossed her eyes. 'Whew! Those women are crazy! How you doin'?'

'What are you doing?' I demanded. 'You're serving refreshments to a bunch of crazies who want me electrocuted?'

MaryNell slipped through the doorway.

'Are you sure about this, Ms Hale?' the policeman asked.

'Oh, yeah, yeah, thanks. She's a nut, but she's OK.'

'If you're sure. I'll be right here.'

'Thanks.'

MaryNell stuck her head back out the door. 'And have some

water, Officer. There's plenty in the basket. It's hot out there.'

'Thank you, ma'am.'

I shut the door.

'What are you doing?'

'How else was I going to get in here without being mobbed? This is my workout T-shirt from my Balance days. I told them I was coming in here to get the truth out of you.' She grinned.

I couldn't stop shaking my head. 'And you brought water? So they won't get hot and tired and give up?'

'And chocolate. Little bars. You throw a whole chocolate cake at them, and they'd run in terror. But mini Hershey bars, fun-size Three Musketeers? They'll start with one, keep munching, and before they know what hit them they'll be producing endorphins and happy with the world.'

'You're drugging them with chocolate?'

MaryNell shrugged. 'Too much deprivation's not good for anybody. It's all about balance. You're live on channel six, you know.'

'I'm what?'

'On TV. I set my VCR. You could watch and see what's going on out there. Like a hostage taker.'

'I don't want to see what's going on out there! I want them to go away.'

'I wouldn't count on it,' MaryNell said. 'That Balance program takes a lot of commitment.'

A knock at the door made us both jump. I looked through the security peephole and turned back to MaryNell. 'Sam.'

'You want me to leave?' she asked.

'No, no. I don't want to talk to him. You should have seen him downtown, acting like he didn't know me. He wouldn't even look at me. I don't think he's here to be supportive. I don't need anybody else yelling at me.'

MaryNell looked out and jumped back at the sound of the second knock. 'You've got to let him in. He's the police. And this is not the time to make them mad. Madder,' she corrected herself.

'Campbell!' he yelled. 'I know you're in there. Open up.'

I didn't say anything.

'I wouldn't want to have to kick this door in to make sure you're all right in there. Probable cause. You called.'

I looked at MaryNell. She shrugged. 'I'd open the door.'

I opened it. But I didn't say anything.

Sam sighed. 'MaryNell.' He nodded as he pushed past me into the room.

She nodded back. 'Sam.'

Those muscles in his jaw were working. I suspected he was grinding his teeth at night. Too much stress. Served him right.

Sandy came running from wherever he'd been hiding, pouting, ignoring me, to rub up against Sam's leg and purr like he'd just found his long-lost best friend. There is no loyalty. Sam bent down absently to rub behind Sandy's ears.

MaryNell spoke first. 'I could leave now. I'll tell them you're sorry.'

'Don't tell them that! I tried to save the woman! I didn't kill her.'

She nodded. 'Yeah, OK. But if I tell them that, they're not going to believe it. And what am I going to tell them about the picture in the paper?'

'Maybe you could leave now.'

'I'll just wing it then.' MaryNell grinned and waved as she left.

I closed and locked the door behind her and watched from the side of the window as she talked to the marchers. I stood sideways, peering around the edge of the window frame, trying not to be seen or offer a target. She shook her head, shrugged, nodded and refused to take the baskets. Then the mother with the baby carrier hugged her, and MaryNell left. Maybe I didn't want to know.

Picture! Oh, yeah, the picture of Fly outside a Freeport bank, a bank that probably offered numbered accounts, accounts identified with long numbers like the one in the legal pad. The legal pad that disappeared in a steamy Miami parking lot.

FORTY-SEVEN

Just an ordinary small town boy
With dreams of a big, wide world
Just an ordinary small town boy
In love with a small town girl

Stick Anderson

I turned to Sam. I looked at him and raised my eyebrows, waiting.

He glared at me. Stalemate.

Finally, Sam said, 'You're OK?'

'No rocks through the windows yet, but my impatiens will never be the same.'

Still glaring, he nodded.

We stood there. I didn't ask him to sit down. I just stood and waited.

Finally he said, 'You wanna' tell me about this?'

'Are you wearing a badge? My attorney told me not to talk to the police unless he was present.'

Those muscles in his jaw were clenching. He looked at me, then the floor, then back at me. He nodded once. 'OK.' He opened the door then stopped and turned back to face me. I could hear the demonstrators shouting outside. 'I'm always wearing a badge.' And he left.

I realized I was shaking I was so mad. And if I let myself cry now I knew it would be loud and wet, and I wouldn't be able to stop until my eyes were swollen and I had a headache. I had to do something. I found the business card Doug had given me. Robert Lee Jefferson. Let me guess, a KA? I punched his number into the phone, maybe a little harder than I had to.

'Jefferson, Jackson and Levy, Law Offices.' The very feminine voice was singsong, pleasant.

'May I speak to Robert Jefferson, please? I'm Campbell Hale.'

'Oh, Miss Hale. We've been expecting your call. Mr Jefferson isn't back in the office yet, but he's talked with Mr Elliott. Mr Elliott's faxed his notes, and the minute Mr Jefferson gets back, he'll look over those and give you a call. Where can he reach you?'

I didn't think I was going anywhere, but I gave her my cell and home numbers.

'That's great. Thank you. And don't worry. Everything's going to be just fine. Mr Jefferson is the best criminal attorney in the state. You're going to be all right.'

I was so pitifully grateful for her reassurance. That's how desperate I was. I wondered how much that cheerful confidence was going to cost me.

Five minutes later the phone rang. 'Miss Hale? Bob Jefferson.' He was calling from a cell phone; I could hear the occasional static. 'Doug Elliott tells me you've got a little problem.'

Then I thought I would lose it. I took a deep, shuddery breath and started to tell my story.

'That's OK, Miss Hale. We'll get into all that later. I'm still about an hour away from the office, so we may not be able to get together today, but I want you to know that I'm on top of this. You just be careful, be smart. If you hear from the police again, you just call me. Don't say a word until I'm with you.' His voice was reassuring, strong, deep, native Nashville, folksy but refined, educated. I could feel myself beginning to relax. 'Have you got a pen handy? You've got my office number; let me give you my home number and my cell number. Don't you hesitate to call me. That's what I'm here for.'

I wrote the numbers he gave me on the back of his card.

He went on. 'You know, I live a block or so from the Youngs. I saw the Balance people marching over there. And Janelle mentioned she'd heard on the news they've been over at your place today. Things OK?'

'Well, they're marching in front of my house. It's this quiet, little neighborhood . . . my neighbors . . . and my flowers;

they tromped all over my impatiens, and they're broken now.'
I really was about to cry now.

'Hmm. OK. We may need to look into a restraining order.
Let's see if they get tired and go home. I'll talk to the TV news
people, we'll make a statement in time for their early
news, see what we can do. I'll get back to you. You just hang
in there, OK? Everything's going to be fine.' And he was gone.

I realized he hadn't asked if I'd murdered Erika.

And I realized I had forgotten to tell Sam about the pictures
of Fly.

I went back to the front windows and saw that only a few
demonstrators were left, and they were leaving. I opened the
door a crack and spoke quietly to the policeman who was still
outside. It suddenly occurred to me to wonder if he was
protecting me or keeping tabs on me.

'Hey.' I hid inside the house as I spoke through the open
door. 'What's going on? I'm not complaining, but why are
they leaving?'

The officer spoke without turning his head toward me. He
even turned his head away, seeming to look at the sky and trees,
talking to himself. I was impressed. I guess he didn't want to
be caught in the mob storming my house if he could help it. 'I
don't know. Right after your friend talked to them, they started
packing up. They seemed to get camera shy all of a sudden.'

'Thanks.' I closed the door and picked up the phone. I hit
the speed dial number for MaryNell. 'MaryNell? What did
you say to them?'

'You know, you don't sound nearly grateful enough. I just
mentioned that baby was looking a little overheated. I suggested
her mother might want to be sure she was OK. And I
suggested she not let the TV people see. It wouldn't look good
if the poor child got heat stroke with the cameras rolling. I
said, "You know how those news people are. First thing you
know, they're talking negligence, interviewing neighbors."
Then I mentioned another child was looking a little hot and
red. Well, who wouldn't be in this heat? They're all crazy, if
you ask me, marching around out there in the sun. So, are
they gone?'

'Yeah, just about.'

'Good. How are *you* doing? You OK?'

'Yeah, sure.' As OK as I can be as a murder suspect, practically a prisoner in my own home, when the man in my life can't bring himself to speak to me.

'Is Sam still there? Did you guys talk things out?'

'No.'

'Ahhh.'

'Yeah.'

'Sorry.'

'Yeah. MaryNell, what if . . .?'

'What?'

'What if . . . I mean, I think, I mean . . .'

'What?'

I couldn't say it. I think Fly Young is still alive. Was I crazy?

'Nothing. Nothing. I don't know. I'm tired. I'll call you later.'

'Campbell! What is it?'

'Nothing. Really. Thanks for getting rid of the marchers. I'll talk to you later. Bye.' I hung up before I could say something I couldn't take back.

I sat down and read the newspaper article again. Where had they gotten that photograph? Who had told them that I had rushed to Miami? And who could have known that I'd had the bag and the laptop and lost them?

I called Mark.

'I need to know where that information came from, Mark.'

'Campbell. I'm sorry, hon. You know I am, but I can't tell you that. I couldn't reveal a source even if it were my own source. I can't do it.'

'But, Mark, it's wrong! Somebody gave that reporter that information, and it's wrong. Somebody's setting me up! And they're using your paper to do it. I'm a murder suspect! Now, who do you think would want me to be a murder suspect?'

'Campbell . . .'

'The murderer!'

'Campbell . . .'

'Think about it. Very few people could know the part of that information that's true. It has to be somebody inside that company. But they'd know the truth. Why would anybody make up the rest of it except to make it look like I killed her? And why would anybody want to do that except the person who really killed her?'

'Campbell.'

'And they won't talk to me. Marcella and the people at HealthwaRx. They had a company meeting and told everybody not to talk to me, not to give me any information.'

'I can tell you who the private investigator is. He's on the record. J.D. Patterson.'

'Do you realize what's at stake here? I'm a murder suspect?'

'Campbell, I don't even know who the source is. No reporter's going to reveal his source. Reporters go to jail rather than do that.'

'Do you have any idea what a criminal attorney is going to cost me?' When he didn't say anything I went on. 'I might have some information to trade.' I still didn't know what to do about my photographs of Fly.

'I'll see what I can find out.' He didn't sound at all promising.

FORTY-EIGHT

I looked in the phone book and found J.D. Patterson Investigations. Retired cop. A recording. 'You've reached J.D. Patterson Investigations. Please leave a number, and I'll call you back. All communication is completely confidential.' That didn't sound too promising either. I left my name and number.

I went back to my computer and opened up the CD with the photos of Freeport. I enlarged the photos with Fly in them and printed them out. I saved them in a file. Suddenly paranoid, I named it 'Christmas family'. I'd probably never find it again.

The phone rang. 'J.D. Patterson.'

'Mr Patterson, I'm Campbell Hale. I—'

'Yes, Ms Hale. I know who you are.'

'Yeah. Well, thanks to your photograph, I'm a murder

suspect. Somebody wants me to be a suspect, and I'm trying to find out who.'

'Can't help you much. I turned my report and photographs over to my client. Erika Young. I wouldn't tell you that much except she's dead. I don't know who she talked to, who she gave 'em to. That's what I told the police. All I told the paper when they called was that I had taken the photograph.'

'You've talked to the police?'

'Yep.'

'What did you tell them?'

'Ms Hale. I've told you all I'm going to. I turned over copies of all my photographs from the case and my report to the police. Both principals are deceased. That's all I can say.'

I recognized a brick wall when I hit one. 'OK. Well, thanks. Thanks for calling me back so quickly.'

'Yes, ma'am.'

'Mr Patterson. One more question.' I barely caught him before he hung up. 'Who did you talk to with the police?'

He laughed. 'Detective Davis. We go way back.'

I tried to decide if that had helped. Patterson had given photographs to Erika. After she's murdered, the photos, or at least one of them, turn up at the newspaper. The police had the P.I. report, so they knew I wasn't having an affair with Fly.

Sam knew I wasn't having an affair with Fly.

How could you get in touch with someone who didn't want to be found?

Fly would probably be checking the *Tennessean* website for news. He'd probably be checking the HealthwaRx and Lifestyle Balance sites, too. If he had Internet access wherever he was. Was he in Nashville? Could he have snuck back into the country? He already had if he was my mugger in Miami. But would he dare come back to Nashville where people knew him? Where his picture was in the newspaper every day?

Had he murdered Erika?

But why? If he were legally dead, he couldn't inherit. If he came back, he'd be a suspect, and there was no statute of limitations for murder. Could it have been an accident? Could he have gone to the house – to see her, to get something, to make some arrangements? She'd have been mad. She'd already been having him followed. Maybe she confronted him with some of what she'd found out or threatened to turn him in. With HealthwaRx stock tanking and cash missing from both companies, she'd have been furious. They could have fought, and she could have hit her head, wound up in the pool without Fly intending to murder her. It could have happened that way.

If that was what happened, what would Fly do?

Would he have planted the false information with the paper? I couldn't see how he could have known all of it.

Unless Marcella or someone else inside the company had been in contact with him, he couldn't have known everything about my being sent to Captain Dave's. Unless Captain Dave had been in touch with him.

The phone rang. 'Hey, Campbell. Mark. I can tell you this much. A manilla envelope was left at the desk downstairs. The photo, with Patterson's name and phone number stamped on it, was inside. No name with it. But the phone numbers of both companies were included. Very helpful. Also a note that the informant would be in touch. The reporter confirmed that you had gone to Florida, gone to the boats, confirmed that you had reported some of the stuff stolen, but no one had seen it happen. Said they tried to reach you for comment. That's all he would tell me. It's the photograph that really makes things look bad for you. Patterson confirmed that he had taken the photograph, didn't say anything else. Nothing that could convict you. All it does is distract the police – and the press – for a couple of days.'

'All it does? Tell that to my mother.'

'Yeah. Sorry. You mentioned some information before. Said you might have some information to trade.'

'Maybe. I haven't figured it out yet.'

'What does that mean?'

'Look, it might be nothing. I don't want to do to somebody else what just happened to me. Let me think about it, figure it out.'

'How 'bout letting me look into it?'

'Not yet.'

I had to think about this a little more first.

Had Fly been setting me up all along? Or had he just been buying himself some time to get back out of the country?

FORTY-NINE

There was a knock at the door. I looked out the security peephole. It was the policeman who had been outside for hours. I opened the door. He was alone.

'You doing OK now, ma'am? Seems like everybody got tired and went home.'

'Yeah, I'm fine.'

'I'm going to leave, then, if you're sure you're OK. We'll have a car coming by every hour or so through the night. If anything happens, you call. OK?'

'Yeah. Sure. Thanks.'

'OK.' He tipped his hat. 'You take care.'

I went back in and turned on the TV. The early evening news was just coming on. Erika's murder was still the lead story, but my name was barely mentioned. I was just the woman who had found Erika. The only film of the marchers outside my house showed MaryNell graciously serving water and chocolate.

I guess I was old news.

I looked at the stack of work I'd brought home. I hadn't touched it yet. I carried it to my computer, piled it on the desk next to me and started to work. I went through the pile methodically.

If I really had seen Fly, if he were alive, how could I contact him? Surely someone was monitoring his email account.

I opened my email program. Except for a home-based business opportunity that would make me millions from my home in less than two hours a day and a site offering legal, organically grown grass, there was nothing new.

I went to my high school site, clicked on Alumni Connections, then the Message Board for the year I had graduated. Melinda had posted her new address. Lots of comments about the recent reunion, thanks to the organizing committee. A few comments about Fly's disappearance, two about the picture of Fly and

me in the paper. Just in case anyone was on the moon and
didn't know yet. Nothing else. I closed the site.

I was about to log off when an instant message popped up.
Want to chat?

I moved the mouse to close it. I never respond to messages
from anyone I don't know. Then I stopped. What if . . .?
What about? I replied. I waited.

**Moonlight on a lake. Dancing, slow and close, to 'A
Whiter Shade of Pale'. A first kiss. Braces. Young love.**

I couldn't breathe. Now what? I put my hand on the phone
to call Sam. Sam who wouldn't talk to me. Sam who knew I
hadn't had an affair with Fly but still wouldn't look me in the
eye. So I typed.

Now what?

Want to chat?

Yes. I have a lot of questions.

☺ **Inquiring minds want to know.**

Where are you?

**Hasn't anyone ever told you not to exchange personal
information with strangers over the Internet?**

I need to talk to you.

I'll be in touch. ☺

And he was gone.

My hands were shaking. It had to be Fly. If Fly was alive,
he was a fraud. Was he also a murderer?

I needed some answers. The only person I could think of
who might know something was Marcella. She wouldn't talk
to me at work, but surely she would tell me what was going
on if I talked to her away from the office, where no one was
watching.

Sandy was looking at me.

'Well, what am I supposed to do? Sit around and wait for
them to take me to jail?'

I typed Marcella's name into a People Search and got her
address. Across town, a condominium on Hillsboro Road in
Green Hills.

FIFTY

I didn't want to sit around wondering what I'd see about myself on the news next, so I locked up, told Sandy to stand guard and headed across town in my little red Spider. I had some questions that I didn't think anyone could answer except Marcella. What really happened to Charlie Patton? Who had given the *Tennessean* reporter information about me? Who didn't want her talking to me and why? Had anyone from the company had an opportunity to be at Erika's house that morning? I knew that Fly's partners, Al Evanston and George Madison, had both been out of the office. What I needed to know was where? Had they really been at the meetings they said they were going to? Would either of them have had time to go to Erika's? And what about Fly? Was he alive? Had he contacted Marcella? Could he be in town? I didn't call ahead because I didn't want to give her a chance to say no. If she weren't home, I'd wait. What else did I have to do except watch my life slip away?

Green Hills Mall looked quiet as I drove past. On a Monday night, the parking lot was relatively empty except near the restaurant entrances. I turned off Hillsboro Road and followed the signs to Marcella's building. I circled, decided which unit was hers and drove around to park in front of another building. I walked back, trying to look like I belonged, taking long, confident strides as if I were just out for the exercise.

I broke stride and went to the door. I pressed the doorbell. I could hear it ringing inside. I waited. Nothing. I rang again. And waited.

She could be gone. I hadn't spotted her car yet.

She could be out walking around the neighborhood like I was pretending to do.

I rang once more, then continued my walk. I circled the complex and saw several people out walking, but not Marcella. I made my way to the alleyway behind Marcella's condominium.

Trashcans and covered parking spaces for residents' cars were hidden behind the units along narrow alleyways. The car at Marcella's back door, a two-year-old Maxima, had a HealthwaRx parking sticker, but she could have left with someone else. In someone else's car.

I rang the bell at the back door. No answer. I looked through a window into Marcella's kitchen and saw her. At least, I thought it was her. I could see her part of her back as she sat in a chair in the next room. Her head leaned against the side of a wingback chair as if she were asleep.

I could knock. Maybe that would be louder than the bell, wake her up.

I rapped on the window of the kitchen door, hard, loud. Marcella didn't move, but the door did. It swung open slightly.

'Marcella?' I called. A little louder. 'Marcella!'

I was beginning to have a bad feeling about this.

'Marcella?' I stepped inside the kitchen. It was clean, very clean. Lights were on in the kitchen but not in the room beyond. 'Marcella?'

The head leaning against the side of the chair didn't stir. I walked across the kitchen slowly, quietly, cautious of what? I stepped into the gloom of what turned out to be a great room, combination living and dining room, and walked around to the front of the chair.

'Marcella?'

Her mouth hung open unattractively. An empty wineglass stood on a side table at her right hand.

'Marcella!' I expected her to wake up, startled, now that I was in her face, but she didn't move. I reached out to touch her arm. It was cool, and the slight movement was enough to make her head fall forward from its spot against the chair's wing. 'Marcella!' I was shouting. I shook her but still no response. 'No, no, not again!'

I put my fingers under her nose to see if she was breathing. I couldn't be sure. I touched the base of her throat, trying to feel a pulse. Maybe. Faint.

I looked around for a phone. At least Erika had had one handy. I was beginning to panic. There! In the kitchen, on the wall. I pushed 911.

'Metropolitan Police. What is your emergency?'

Not again.

It seemed like hours before I heard sirens, but I know it was only minutes. I decided I was really going to have to take a refresher course in CPR if I was going to keep this up. Maybe get one of those mouthpieces, keep it in my purse.

This time when the paramedic took over and eased me out of the way, I slumped down on the floor against the living room wall and sobbed. Within minutes uniformed policemen were around me, asking questions, but all I could do was sob. I couldn't even catch my breath to speak.

'Get her some water, do you think?' I heard someone say. 'She's in shock.'

'Anybody call Davis?'

'Yeah, he's on the way.'

I was vaguely aware of the paramedics wheeling Marcella out on a stretcher through the blur of faces and sounds around me. Then I heard Sam's voice.

'Campbell! Campbell! It's OK. Campbell!' Was someone shaking me, or was it just me? 'I'm gonna pay for this later.' Smack!

He slapped me! Sam slapped me!

Then I realized I was staring at him, still sobbing and choking, and clutching his jacket lapels in both hands.

'Campbell.' His voice was soft, calming now. 'Campbell, it's OK.'

'Sam! I didn't kill her. I didn't do anything. Is she OK? Is she dead?'

'Hey. You're OK. Settle down.'

I flung myself against his chest, and, reluctant or not, he put his arms around me and patted my back for all the world as if I were five years old. I cried, and he patted, and finally I stopped. A glass of water appeared in a hand extending from a dark blue cuff. I took it, sat back to drink and realized Sam and I were in a circle of dark blue uniforms.

'Breathe,' he said. 'Just breathe. In and out.' He took off his jacket and put it around me. Light gleamed off the blue gray gun in the worn leather shoulder holster. 'Can you stand up now? We need to get outside, let these guys do their job.'

Sam helped me up and kept his arm around me as we went back through the kitchen and out the door. Outside, I took a deep breath of air, humid and heavy with the scent of some sweet, decaying flower. I threw up. All over the shrub at the side of Marcella's door.

'You want me to get her some more water?' I heard a voice ask.

'Not from in there. We've screwed around in there enough. Maybe one of these neighbors standing around.'

When I caught my breath, Sam was holding wet paper towels. A uniformed officer beside him held out a paper cup of water.

'Here,' Sam said. 'Let's move away from the door. You sure have a way of messing up crime scenes.'

I tried to clean myself up. Crime scene investigators were taping boundaries, taking photographs.

'Campbell!'

I looked up to see Doug. 'How did you . . .?'

Sam spoke to him. 'You'll meet us downtown?'

Doug nodded.

Sam looked at me and shook his head.

Doug led me to his car. I realized I still had Sam's jacket. 'Why . . .? How did you . . .? Who called you?' I finally got out.

He started the car, turned off his air conditioning as it came on. I realized I was still shivering. 'Officially, nobody. I was passing by.'

'Sam called you?'

'Don't ask. Everybody knows homicide detectives don't call suspects' attorneys for them. Bobby Jefferson's on his way. He'll meet us downtown.' I didn't say anything. 'Look, they don't think you did this. But somebody's doing a good job of making you the patsy. Listen to Bobby, do whatever he says, but I think he's going to tell you to tell them what you know, whatever you saw. But don't do it alone. You don't say anything until he gets there. And if he tells you to stop, you stop.'

I nodded. Was it time to show someone the pictures from Freeport? I knew it was. Of course, it was. But I couldn't believe Fly was a murderer. I wanted a chance to talk to him first.

FIFTY-ONE

I was beginning to know the Criminal Justice Center way too well. People who worked there recognized me, knew me to nod to. I knew where the Coke machines were. But this time I needed coffee, strong, hot and black.

A uniformed woman brought me some in a Styrofoam cup. I burned my tongue on the first sip, so it didn't matter how it tasted. 'You need anything else?' she asked.

An alibi? I shook my head.

Bobby Jefferson arrived at the station downtown just minutes after Doug and I did. Doug stayed to hear me tell Bobby what had happened, then patted me on the shoulder and left. 'I wouldn't mind going a week without hearing about you and a dead body,' he said on his way out.

Yeah, me, too.

Bobby was reassuring. 'OK, just tell them what happened the same way. Our position is, you're cooperating, you haven't done anything wrong, you just want to help the police find whoever's doing this.'

'Well, yeah!'

'Right, right. I think we stick with that, tell them whatever you can remember. If I think we're getting into anything that could be trouble, I'll stop you.'

FIFTY-TWO

The bright fluorescent lights were harsh; they sucked the life and color out of everything in the room. I hated to think what I looked like. I'd given CPR to yet another nearly dead person, had my face in a shrub, thrown up. A faint scent made me think I hadn't kept Sam's jacket entirely out of the way. I wanted to be home. Sam still hadn't shown up. Bobby Jefferson and I sat alone at a long table that filled the bright, depressing room.

I told Bobby what I had done, what I'd seen, and he took me back through the story, step by step.

'When was the last time you talked to her?' he asked. I told him. 'And exactly what did she say?' I tried to reconstruct the conversation. He nodded. 'And exactly why did you go to see her, at home, unannounced?'

'Because somebody's trying to set me up for murder, and I thought she could tell me who!' I was tired. I was angry. I was coming out of emotional shock, and I had no patience left. I continued ranting as Sam and his team came into the room. 'Because someone didn't want her to talk to me, and I wanted to know why. Because she's the only one I know who can tell me who Erika was seeing the morning she was killed! Because she's the only one I know who might be able to tell me who from the HealthwaRx office talked to the *Tennessean* yesterday!'

Sam and the other detectives found chairs around the table.

'And whoever that was got to her first!'

I downed the last of the coffee in my cup, swallowing it before I realized it was cold now, the consistency of sludge and about as tasty.

Sam spoke first. 'I think we all need a fresh cup.' He nodded at a uniformed officer standing by the door, who left and returned with a tray of cups of coffee. I noticed that most of the officers grimaced as they drank it.

'OK.' Sam nodded to another officer who set a recorder on the table and turned it on. Sam stated his name, the date, time, place and the names of everyone in the room. 'Campbell. Just start at the beginning and tell us what happened.'

Bobby Jefferson interrupted before I could say anything. 'Just one thing. For the record.' He pointedly spoke toward the recorder. 'My client is cooperating fully and willingly, even eagerly. She wants the perpetrator of these crimes found and found quickly. She feels, and I wholeheartedly agree with her, that she, too, is a victim, and that her best interests will be served by the expeditious resolution of these crimes. For the record.'

Sam nodded. 'Campbell?' His voice was neutral. That helped.

'What about Marcella? Is she alive?'

He shook his head.

'What was it? How did they do it?'

'We're working on that.'

I took a deep breath and started. I told them how I'd called Marcella at work and she'd said she'd been told not to talk to me. I left out the Freeport photos. For now. Sam, Bobby and the others made notes, but no one spoke until I had finished. Then we started again. What time did I arrive at Marcella's? How long had I rung the front door bell? Why had I parked in front of another building? And why, again, had I walked around the neighborhood before trying the back door? Whom had I seen while I was pretending to be out walking? Every time I spoke, a tableful of calm, level eyes focused on me. Then pens and pencils scribbled. The adrenaline wore off; the caffeine wore off, and I didn't have much else left.

'Can I go home now?'

Sam looked around the table, his eyebrows raised in question. Paul Green gestured with his hand to indicate that he didn't have any more questions. A couple of other officers shook their heads. Everyone began to stand, pick up notepads, pens, coffee cups.

'Your car's back at the condominium in Green Hills?' Bobby Jefferson asked. I nodded. 'I'll give you a lift,' he said.

'Thanks.'

He looked from me to Sam. 'I'll wait out here.' He walked out of the room and down the hallway, leaving Sam and me alone in the room.

I turned to Sam. 'I'll get your jacket cleaned.'

He shrugged. 'You OK?'

'No. No, I'm not. What have you found out about Charles Patton's murder?'

Sam shook his head. 'I can't talk about that.'

'You don't think it's a coincidence.' So why are you wasting your time with me, I wanted to ask. 'Why are you wasting your time with me?'

'Would it do any good for me to tell you to stay home, not put yourself in dangerous situations?'

'You're saying this is all my fault?'

Sam shook his head, a disgusted look on his face. 'I've got men patrolling your house.'

'They're too late for my impatiens.'

Sam held the door, and I left.

FIFTY-THREE

'd have died before I'd have let Sam know, but I was glad he had officers patrolling my street. One step behind a murderer – twice! – was too close for me.

The first thing I did – after I deadbolted the doors and checked the locks on every window – was turn on my computer and check my email. Nothing exciting.

I put food out for Sandy and cleaned and refilled his water dish. Sandy watched from a safe distance. I decided to wait for him to speak first. He kept his peace, so I went back to the computer. I checked some websites, the *Tennessean*, the *New York Times*, Parnassus, the Square Books site, looking for books on banks in the Caribbean that offered numbered accounts. A news item about Marcella's death was already on the *Tennessean* site. Very brief. They called it an unexplained death, not a murder, and said police were investigating a possible connection to Erika Young's murder.

Then it happened, and I knew what I had been waiting for. An instant message popped onto the screen.

What's happening?

I reminded myself to breathe.

You tell me.

Well, there's the problem. I don't know.

What are you saying? Who does?

Nothing happened. I waited. Then a message appeared.

I assume you haven't been on a killing spree?

I wondered if there was a little emoticon face for murderous rage. *No, but keep talking. You might inspire me.*

☺ **Nice to see you haven't lost your sense of humor. I've always loved that about you.**

I want to know what's going on!

You, me and the police, too, I imagine. I'm thinking the key is whoever planted the information with the Tennessean. I have an idea, but nothing to support it. If I show up, the investigating stops. You know that's true.

He was right. If Fly turned up alive now, he'd be arrested, of course, but no one would believe that he was innocent.

Did I?

Sort of.

Right now I didn't have much choice. I could show Sam the photos, but that wouldn't tell us where Fly was now. If he had murdered Erika and Marcella, all he had to do was disappear again. And if he were going to kill Erika, why go to all the trouble of faking his death first? If he were declared dead, he couldn't inherit. If he reappeared, he'd go to prison on several counts of fraud. So either his plan had gone very wrong or Erika's death had never been part of Fly's plan. I wanted to believe that.

I suppose you're right. Now what?

Can you find out who gave the Tennessean the information?

No. I've tried. I even have a close friend there, but the reporter won't reveal his source.

What if you had something to trade?

Like what?

There was another pause.

A picture from Freeport?

So it was Fly! And he had seen me that day. Was he really suggesting I turn him in to get information from the reporter? Or was he trying to find out if I had the photo so he could steal it? Or keep me from using it?

Another message appeared.

Your call.

The instant message screen disappeared.

I paced the house, leaving the computer on and checking the screen each time I passed. No other messages appeared.

OK. It was time. I called Mark. It was late. I got his voicemail.

I left a message.

'I have something to trade that I think your buddy will be interested in. I want to know who gave him the information, everything he knows about it. What I have is worth it.'

Then I worked on insurance.

FIFTY-FOUR

I had ordered double prints and a CD when I left the film. I put prints of the two pictures showing Fly and the front of the bank in an envelope. I included a note with the date and location of the photograph, where I'd had the prints made and a statement that I hadn't known what was in the photos until I picked up the prints. I addressed the envelope to Bobby Jefferson, sealed it and put it beside my purse to mail when I went out.

I went back to the computer. I opened the CD with the photos and attached the two that mattered to an email message to Doug with the same information I had put in the letter to Bobby. I entered a command to send all email messages in my outbox at six p.m. the next day.

What about Sam?

I had to tell Sam, but, if I told him first, he wouldn't let me make my trade and find out who was trying to set me up. He'd go after Fly, and it would be a long time, if ever, before anybody looked in any other direction. I'd have to think about that.

I sealed the CD in a Ziploc bag and buried it at the bottom of the large tin where I stored Sandy's cat food.

That left me with one set of prints to give Mark and the reporter. I might need more. I dug the CD out of the cat food, nasty smelling stuff, and copied it. One more instant message appeared then disappeared quickly while I was working.

Be careful.

That was all.

Then I put the CD copy back in my hiding place.

I sat at the kitchen table looking out at the river and waited for Mark to call. Sandy came over and curled up against my ankle.

I tried to read while I waited for Mark to call, but I couldn't concentrate. I mostly stared out the window into blackness. The phone rang twice, but the calls were from my mother and MaryNell. I didn't want to tell either of them what I was about to do. Both of them would tell me it was too dangerous. So I made small talk and listened for the call waiting beep.

Finally I gave up and went to bed.

FIFTY-FIVE

Mark called at six thirty the next morning.

'What are you talking about?' he asked.

'I need to know who gave you guys that information. Because whoever it was is probably the person who killed Erika, probably the person who killed Marcella, and definitely the person who wants me to look really bad.'

'If you're right, you don't want to meet him.'

'If I'm right, he already knows who I am, but he could knock at my door and I wouldn't know unless somebody tells me who he is.'

'Look, I talked to the reporter. He really doesn't know. I can put you in touch with him, but he has no contact, no phone number. The guy left the information in an envelope at the reception desk. The guy's called him a few times since. No caller ID, probably calling from a public phone, maybe a burner.'

'Well, here's the deal. I have something your guy's going to want. Something everybody's going to want. Huge. But your guy doesn't get it unless I find out who his source is. You figure it out.'

Mark sighed. 'What am I supposed to do?'

'I don't know. Wait for the police news conference?'

'What have you got?'

'Just between us?'

He sighed again. 'OK. Just between us.'

'Franklin Young is alive. I have pictures.'

'What?'

'Franklin Young is alive.'

'How do you know?'

'I took his picture. I didn't know it until I got around to getting my prints made, but I happened to get two shots of him coming out of an international bank in Freeport. He saw me.'

'You're serious.'

'Serious as being framed for two murders.'

'You think he did it?'

'No. I don't. I can't figure out why he would disappear and then do it. If he turns up alive, he loses his alibi. If he doesn't, he can't collect insurance or inherit. No. I don't think he did it.'

'It's not just somebody who looks like him? Happens all the time. You're traveling and you see somebody who looks like somebody at home.'

'I've got pictures. You decide.'

'OK.' He didn't sound happy about it. 'I'll get back to you.'

FIFTY-SIX

I went back to work that morning. I had to take the reservation system down and reboot my computer. It was locked up. Something the police had done to it. I didn't get much work done. I kept waiting for Mark to call.

The postman came and took away my package for Bobby Jefferson.

I was in the middle of arranging a honeymoon in the Dominican Republic when he finally did call. 'Great beach,' I was saying. 'Really beautiful beach. I think bugs are bad there that time of year. You'll want to take some bug spray along. But it's great value. It's funny. Not many Americans go there, but you'll see a lot of Europeans.'

'Campbell,' Anna whispered. 'It's Mark. He says it's very important.'

I mouthed 'thanks' to her. 'Can I call you right back?' I asked the client. 'Sure, right. OK. Thanks.' I pressed the button with the blinking light.

'What's up?' I asked.

'Will you show me the pictures?'

'Of course.'

'OK. The guy said he'd call back in a couple of days. Could be today. The reporter's going to try to set up a meeting. You can be where you can see. Thing is, we need something to get the guy there. Like your pictures.'

'No offense, Mark, but it sounds like a bad deal for me.'

'I told him you'd say that. How about we make a couple of color copies of your photos? Or email them to me? The resolution's going to be bad, nothing the paper could use, but enough to show our guy, enough to get him out in the open.'

'OK.'

'The thing is, you have to stay out of sight.'

'Why?'

'Because I think you might be right. And if you are, this guy is a killer who already doesn't like you. He knows who you are, so you can't hope he won't recognize you. It's too dangerous.'

'Well, we can figure it out once it's set up.'

'I'll see you in a little bit.'

I called two wholesalers and got competitive bids for the honeymoon while I waited. I got prices for the Dominican Republic resort, an all-inclusive in Cancun, a couple in the Bahamas. One of them was a resort I'd visited in Freeport the day I took the pictures of Fly.

FIFTY-SEVEN

When Mark walked in, everybody stopped working and watched. How long would it be before we could see Mark or Sam or even Doug walk in the door and not expect a tragedy? He nodded to everyone but didn't waste time on small talk.

I pulled out the prints and handed them to him. His eyes got big, and he nodded. 'OK. Can you make me some copies?'

I got up, and he followed me to the copier.

'I'm not so sure your old boyfriend's not the killer,' Mark said while we waited for it to warm up.

'He's the one who suggested I trade his photos for a chance to find out who is.'

'What do you mean?'

Oh, yeah. I grimaced. I hadn't meant to say anything about the instant message emails.

'What do you mean?' Mark repeated.

I could just refuse to say anything.

Mark pulled me around to face him. 'I'm not going anywhere until you tell me what you're talking about.'

'OK. I got these instant messages last night. No name, but it was Fly. He knew some things nobody but Fly could know.'

'Oh, yeah?' Mark leered. 'Tatoos, preferences, that kind of thing?'

'No. *Not* that kind of thing. Just stuff.'

The leer remained.

'You can just wipe that look off your face, or I don't tell you another thing.'

Mark grinned. He ran his hand across his face, but the grin stayed. 'So you've been getting emails from the guy half the people in the state think is dead and the other half is looking for, not to mention the Coast Guard, the Securities and Exchange Commission and the Justice Department.'

'You make it sound like it's been going on for a long time. It was last night.'

He held up both hands. 'I don't want to know. I don't want to be an accessory after the fact.'

'You asked.'

'One day I'll learn.'

'Anyway,' I said, 'he knows this means he's busted. It seems he faked his own death. He may very well have embezzled from his wife, his partners and his shareholders, but I don't believe he's a murderer.'

'Money's a pretty big motive,' he said. Mark didn't look convinced, but he settled down. He made enlarged, fuzzy copies and picked them up off the tray. He was right. They were too fuzzy for the paper to reproduce, but Fly was still clearly recognizable in them. Mark took the copies; I kept the photos.

'How bad is the guy's luck?' Mark said. 'I mean, he grows a beard, he's in a different country, he hadn't even seen you for twenty years until a few weeks before. Then there you are with a camera pointed right at him. You couldn't have done it if you'd been trying.'

'Yeah.' Should I be insulted?

'And, this isn't the kind of thing you do on the spur of the moment. He's been planning this for months, years, maybe, and everything works out just fine until somebody starts killing everyone he knows. Almost like somebody was waiting for his chance.'

I nodded. Something Mark had just said was nagging at me. Almost making a connection. I was still trying to figure out what it was when Mark went out the door.

If Fly had been planning this, was his showing up at the reunion part of the plan? Had he planned all along to use me somehow? Or, if I hadn't been almost involved with Sam, would he have asked me to come along? I was definitely out of my depth.

I jumped every time my phone rang the rest of the day, but Mark didn't call. I didn't hear from him until after I'd slogged my way through the afternoon drive home. I noticed the impatiens were trampled and crushed. The blooms were dead, but maybe some new growth would grow from the breaks in the stems. I could thank the Balance women for the pruning. Right.

I checked the messages as soon as I got inside. Nothing.

It was past six, so my email had gone to Doug. I was pretty sure he wouldn't see it before morning, though.

It was past six thirty when Mark called. 'No word yet.'

'Great.'

'There is something on the woman who died last night, though. It could have been natural causes.'

'Are you kidding?'

'No. She was diabetic. She had apparently gone into diabetic shock. It'll take a while for toxicology reports to come back, but that's what it looks like. It looks like she'd had some wine. That could have been a factor; stress can be a factor. She's on medication, but if she took too much, if some of these other things affected her system . . . It happens.'

I didn't know what to say. I really did hope Marcella hadn't been murdered, but how much of a coincidence was that? What was it Sam always said? It's not that he doesn't believe in coincidence, but it sure does make him suspicious. Me, too.

'So what next?'

'They're waiting on more tests. Some of those toxicology tests can take six, eight weeks to turn around. They haven't made a finding yet, but you may be off the hook.'

'You mean I may not be a murderer? I may just be bad luck?'

'Pretty much.'

I thought Sam might call to tell me about Marcella, but he didn't. And Mark didn't call back.

MaryNell called to ask me to come over for supper.

'Thanks, but I need to stick around home.'

'Why? You expecting more demonstrators?'

'I sure hope not.'

'OK. So why?' MaryNell demanded. 'You've got something going on, haven't you? Is Sam coming over?'

'No. Sam's not even speaking. Something tells me Sam may never be coming over again.'

'I doubt that. Sam's solid. He doesn't strike me as the kind of man to let a couple of murders stand in his way.'

'Thanks. That's encouraging. And it looks like Marcella wasn't murdered.'

'Really! Why?'

'She was diabetic. Went into shock.'

'How do they know this? They've talked with her doctor?'

'I guess. Mark told me.'

'Well. That's awful, but it lets you off the hook.'

'I guess.'

'So, we'll see you about six thirty?'

'No. Really. I'm staying in tonight.'

'Then what's going on?'

'Goodbye, MaryNell.'

'If you go to another murder tonight, can I go, too?'

I hung up.

FIFTY-EIGHT

It was Wednesday night before I heard from Mark again. He wasn't happy.

'I don't feel good about this, but the meeting is set for tomorrow night, eight thirty at the Wildhorse, main floor, to the left of the stage. You can get there ahead of time and wait on the second or third floor. Out of sight. You can see who comes without being seen. But be careful. Don't hang over the rail. Remember the idea is that nobody sees you.'

I knew what he meant. The Wildhorse Saloon on Second Avenue is neo-Western Rustic, three levels of tables around a dance floor. There's a stage and usually live entertainment. It would be crowded, but with tourists and twenty-somethings, probably not people who'd know either of them. Or me. If someone did happen to recognize either man, it wouldn't look suspicious. Public place. And I could lurk upstairs without ever being seen.

'That sounds great. I'll be there. Thanks.'

'Yeah, but the reporter wants the photos then.'

'Sure. OK. I'll bring them with me.'

Wednesday night I had another message from Fly. I was trying to stay busy, accomplish something, but I kept my computer on and kept checking it.

Any news?

Not yet.

Nobody interested in your vacation photos?

It wasn't a vacation.

Sorry. Touchy?

I ignored that.

There is interest. I'm working on it.

Any news about Charlie?

Nothing.

I never intended anything like this.

I wanted to believe that.

I know.

And then I had to ask.

What did you intend?

Nothing. I waited.

Looking for that sunset.

FIFTY-NINE

I went to work on Thursday, but I didn't get much done. Lee, Martha and Anna all covered for me. They screened my calls and only passed on ones they thought I had to handle immediately.

The *Tennessean* was reporting that Marcella had apparently died from natural causes. Al Evanston confirmed that she had indeed been on hypoglycemic medication for years. He had been her personal physician from the days before HealthwaRx when Marcella had managed his practice. The medical examiner confirmed that the results of his examination were consistent with diabetic shock. Evanston's statement went on to deplore the 'recent events that had caused stress for Marcella, for all

of us. I hold the person responsible for those events,' he said,
'responsible for Marcella's death as well. She didn't deserve
this. And we're all going to miss her.'

Mark came by at lunchtime. We walked across the street
and had sandwiches while he went over the plan again.

'The main thing,' he insisted, 'is for you to be safe. Stay
out of sight. Don't take any chances.'

I nodded.

'Look,' he said. 'You don't have to go. We can have
somebody follow him, check a license plate. We'll figure out
who he is. It may just take a while.'

'No. I'm going. I may recognize him. I'm going to be there.'

Mark looked glum. 'I figured you'd say that.'

He made sure I understood the details. He walked back
across the street with me and left me at the office door. 'Just
be careful.'

'Of course.'

Still no word from Sam. I was glad. I knew I should have
told him about the photos already, but I didn't want to say
anything until after tonight's meeting.

SIXTY

Sandy knew something was up. He was waiting for me
when I got home, sitting there, watching the front door.
'Hungry?' I asked. He didn't answer. I went to the
kitchen and put out fresh food and water. 'How's that?' He had
followed me to the kitchen, but he ignored his dinner. 'What?'

Sandy just drummed the wooden floor with his tail.

'I'll be careful. What can go wrong? I'm not going to meet
the guy. I'm not even going to talk to him. I'm just going to
watch. From afar.'

Sandy turned and walked out of the room.

It might not be a bad idea to have some police backup. I
could call Sam, maybe ask him to meet me downtown. I picked
up the phone and started to dial his number. Unless I told him

why, though, he probably wouldn't come. He certainly didn't seem to want to see me these days.

I hung up and went to my room to change clothes. Jeans, I decided, a white T-shirt, a faded denim shirt open over it. Nashville camouflage. Nothing to draw attention. Twisted my hair up in a clasp. I didn't want to be noticed tonight.

I was at the door and about to leave when I remembered that I still hadn't said anything to Sam, to the police, about the photos. I really should do that before handing them over to the press. I went to my computer, pulled up sent emails and copied the one I had sent to Doug. I addressed it to Sam, started to send it, then decided to add a little more insurance. I told Sam the name of the file in my computer where I had saved the photos, where I was hiding the CD and the name of the reporter I was going to hand the photos over to. I started to add something personal, but what? I didn't have time to think of the right thing to say. He probably wouldn't check his email before tomorrow anyway. By then I would have called to give him the identity of his murderer. I hit send.

SIXTY-ONE

Even on a Thursday night, Second Avenue was packed. It looked like there was a concert at the Arena. Finding a parking place was not going to be easy. I drove up Second, dodging the crowds crossing back and forth across the street, spilling off the sidewalks. I couldn't circle too many times looking for a spot; there's a cruising law now for downtown. You can be ticketed if you pass the same spot more than twice. I saw a car pulling out of a lot two blocks north of the Wildhorse. I whipped in and took the space it had left at the back of the lot.

The lot stretched between Second and First with Fort Nashborough and the Cumberland River beyond. It wouldn't be parking space for long. Sooner or later, a developer would erect a high rent building here. First Avenue ran between the

Cumberland River and the back doors of the Second Avenue buildings, the ones that are still there after the Christmas Day bombing. Down where Broadway dead-ended at the river, the city had developed Riverfront Park in the narrow strip between the street and the water. Concrete terraces stepped up from the bank to make seating for summer concerts. North of the park was Fort Nashborough, a replica of the first settlement here, a wooden stockade where docents demonstrated pioneer survival skills for school children and tourists.

Tonight, though, there was just darkness beyond the parking lot. Parking alone downtown was not something I would normally do, and I never liked parking my Spider in out-of-the-way spaces. I locked the door, slipped the shoulder strap of my bag over my head and tried to blend in with the crowd on the street and look like I was walking purposefully back down the street toward the Wildhorse.

I paid the cover charge and headed upstairs. I decided the second level was high enough. I found a table where I could see the entrance and ordered club soda and an appetizer, fried zucchini strips. I ordered for cover, but I realized I was hungry. I went through it pretty fast and asked for a second one for cover.

I was there a full hour early, careful not to risk arriving at the same time as Mark's reporter friend or his contact. Matte Gray's band was onstage. It was going to be a long hour, but at least there would be good music.

'Hey, lady, you alone?'

I jumped. Oh, great. Now some guy tries to pick me up. I looked up. Mark. 'Hi.'

'Hey.' He grinned. 'You undercover?'

'Apparently not far enough under.'

'See the third table from the front, just under the balcony on the other side?'

I looked and saw a man sitting there alone. 'Yep.'

Mark nodded. 'That's the reporter, Tom. You ready to hand over the photos?'

'Yeah, but I want to know who the guy is. If he doesn't show or something goes wrong, you all still have to help me find out.'

'Deal.'

'OK.' I pulled the pictures out of my purse and handed them to Mark.

'Thanks. I'd stay with you, but I've got to get these over to the paper. They're holding space.'

'Tonight?'

He looked sheepish.

'It's going to be in tomorrow's paper?'

He nodded.

Sam wasn't going to like that. And it wasn't going to make him much happier when he opened his email and saw that I'd sent the information to him too late for him to know before the press. I decided I'd call him when I left here. With any luck, that would be less than an hour from now.

I shrugged.

'See you,' Mark said. 'Be careful.'

I nodded.

SIXTY-TWO

I remember when we were eighteen
Everything was out there and waiting
On the top of our world, our very small world
We'd found everything that mattered
You and me, when we were eighteen

Stick Anderson

I watched Mark leave, saw him appear downstairs and walk out the door. I moved so I was in the shadows but could still see the table where the reporter sat.

I waited, growing numb from the noise. Eight o'clock came and went. The reporter sat patiently. A waitress stopped at my table. 'You need another one?'

I looked up. 'No, thanks. I'm OK.' I hoped I wouldn't be here long enough for another.

I looked back, and saw a man approaching the table. He circled the table to sit down, and my mouth fell open. Al Evanston! Fly's partner! What had Fly said? We used to be best friends, but things change? Marcella had said Erika was pressuring Al and George for money that wasn't there. But Marcella was dead now, so she couldn't confirm that. And where had the money gone? There was no sense of money missing until after Fly was missing. Had Fly really taken it without anyone suspecting, or had Al taken advantage of Fly's disappearance to embezzle cash and blame it on Fly? Should I call Sam now?

The reporter pulled the color copies out of his jacket and showed them to Evanston. Evanston sat back, looked shocked. Afraid? Afraid that Fly was the one person who could incriminate him? Now that he'd killed Erika and Marcella was dead, too. And Al Evanston was the one who knew all about Marcella's history of diabetes. Al Evanston had been her physician, had known what medication she was on – and how much.

Enough. I hit Sam's number on my cell phone speed dial.

'Sam, this is Campbell.' This wasn't going to be easy.

'Where are you?'

I could barely hear him. The band was taking a break, but I knew he could hear the noise of the club. 'I'm at the Wildhorse. Al Evanston killed Erika.'

'How do you know?' His voice was level, polite.

'It's a long story. I sent you an email that explains part of it. Fly Young is alive.'

'Yeah?' He didn't sound entirely shocked, but I went on.

'I took a picture of him in Freeport, but I didn't know it until now, well, until a couple of days ago, and I knew whoever talked to the *Tennessean* and tried to implicate me had to be the one who killed her. Nobody else had a reason to.' I took a breath. 'So I set him up.'

'You wha—'

'I traded the photographs of Fly to the reporter in exchange for finding out who he was. They're meeting right now downstairs. I'm looking at them right now.'

'Don't move. Stay right where you are. I'm on my way.'

'No. I'm fine. He can't see me. He has no reason to suspect anything. I'll just wait until they leave and go home.'

'Campbell! Wait there. I'm sending an officer in to take you home.'

'No. I'm fine! I just wanted you to know what's going on. Don't worry about me. Pick up Al Evanston.'

While I was speaking, Al and the reporter stood. The reporter laid a bill on the table, and the two left.

'Campbell, don't be stupid.'

'I've got to go now. Call me after you've looked at the email, OK?' I disconnected.

I tried to get the waitress's attention. She didn't look my way, so I left enough cash for the check and tip and made my way downstairs. I wasn't hurrying. I wanted to make sure I didn't run into Al. I looked around, making sure he wasn't in sight. I hesitated again before going out the door, then walked fast. The street was still crowded, so I didn't feel threatened. Until I got to the parking lot. It was dark, and the space I'd found was at the back of the lot, too far from the walking crowds. I walked straighter, faster.

I was steps from my car when I heard him. Before it registered and my brain could send a message to my body to react, he had me. He'd grabbed both arms and pinned me suddenly. Had Al Evanston seen me after all, or was this a random mugging? I twisted to look and saw George Madison!

He wrapped one arm tightly around me and with his other hand stuffed something in my mouth, jamming it deep into my throat. I choked and gagged.

I had my keys in my hand just like you're supposed to. If I had a new car instead of my '65 Alfa Spider, I could hit a panic button on the key fob, make noise.

'It's too bad, really, another young woman, drinking too much, out alone on a dangerous city street. A sad statistic. We'll just step over here, across the street to the river. We'll look like a couple, a little romantic, a little drunk. No one will notice.'

I couldn't argue with him, couldn't try to be logical. I couldn't speak. I tried to kick. I tried to scream, but only grunts came out, and that choked me more. He was pushing me past my car into the street. My phone rang. It rang until the voicemail kicked in, then started again. Probably Sam. I should have taken him up on the escort. I kept trying to kick Madison, but I wasn't connecting much, and that kept me more off balance. He kept pushing me across the street toward the riverbank. Where were all the homeless who were supposed to hang out around here? Why could you never find a homeless person when you needed one?

I heard sirens behind me on Second. Did they have anything to do with me? *If you get me out of this, God, I will never, ever come downtown alone at night.*

'It's a shame, really,' Madison was saying. 'You're the best travel agent we've had.'

Once he got me across the street and down the bank, no one would see me. There'd be nothing to keep Madison from dumping me in the river. It was getting harder to breathe now, harder to think. My phone kept ringing intermittently.

'So many sad events.' He was struggling, trying to hold on to me. 'First Charlie. It's just not a safe world anymore. Erika and poor Marcella. Never careful enough about her medicine, her diet.' He laughed. 'Lucky thing Young wandered into that storm. He was beginning to be a bother. If he'd just stuck to his little computer programs, we'd all be fine.'

I suddenly remembered the last time I'd been with my toddler nephew. It was time to leave the playground, and he didn't want to go. He had gone limp, just dropped, a dead weight, and I couldn't move this three-year-old. I was at the far side of First Avenue now, and it was my last chance. I dropped, going as limp as I could.

It almost worked. It did throw him off balance for a second. There were more sirens now. I could see blue lights flashing off cars and buildings a block away on Second. Madison was already grunting and out of breath from pushing and dragging me. When he realized what I was doing, he cursed, freed one hand and hit me. His fist hit the side of my head, and I saw light. Seeing stars, that's what they meant. You really do see stars. It made me feel dizzy. And he was still moving me toward the riverbank.

Sam, Sam, where are you? You always show up to rescue

me, but I'm running out of time. Out of the corner of my eye, I saw Madison's hand coming toward me again as he bent over me, and this time he held a brick.

This time the light was brighter; the pain was blinding, and everything went black. I heard a splash before I felt the water, breathed in the dirty Cumberland water, and that was all.

SIXTY-THREE

Do you remember . . .
The stars in the sky . . .
Our dreams for tomorrow . . .
A faith in forever . . .
The night's last goodbye . . .
Do you remember?

Stick Anderson

The next thing I knew – and I remember being immediately and profoundly grateful there was a next thing – I was coughing, choking and throwing up all over a white-shirted paramedic. Oh, man. This was happening way too often.

Lights were flashing, blue, red, yellow, white; sirens were blasting, and my head was killing me. And I felt my eyes go wide in panic. Fire engines?

'Ma'am, you're OK. We're going to give you a little oxygen. You're OK.' He was putting a brace around my neck. I realized I was on a back board. Another hand was attaching EKG stickers.

Another EMS was tucking a blanket around me. I was shivering.

'Can I talk to her yet?' I couldn't see a face behind the voice. The lights around me and in my head were blinding me.

'Give her a minute. You catch the guy?'

I felt a sudden sharp pain on the back of my hand and looked to find an IV tube extending from it.

'Not yet.'

'Madison.' I choked it out.

'What?' The paramedic and a uniformed police officer leaned close.

I put a lot of effort into speaking. It came out barely understandable. 'George Madison.'

The policeman stepped away, spoke into the microphone clipped to his uniform, then returned.

'This the woman who was in the paper last week?' the paramedic asked.

I didn't hear an answer.

'You make her for the Young woman's killer? My wife did that Balance thing. She was ready to string her up.'

Great. Just what you want to hear from the paramedic who holds your life in his hands.

The other voice answered. 'Doubt it. We think that's why she ended up in the river.'

The voice with the blanket was softer, a woman. 'OK, now, we're going to get you in the ambulance.'

Nausea swept through me with the motion.

'Let me look in your eyes, hon.' Another light. In one eye, then the other. 'It may not just be the water. She may have a concussion.'

I closed my eyes. And that made me feel sick, too.

SIXTY-FOUR

I don't want to think about the rest of that night. They put me in an ambulance, and the noise just got worse. It's not far from Second Avenue to St Thomas Hospital Midtown: eighteen, nineteen blocks to the emergency entrance. But between the noise and the pain in my head, the trip seemed to take forever. It felt so safe to be there in the emergency room, being wheeled in the automatic doors to welcoming, smiling nurses. It felt almost like coming home.

'OK, honey, let's just get your vitals here. Then we'll get you out of those wet clothes. We've got this nice, dry hospital gown. Designer label, it's got St Thomas Hospital stamped on it.' She laughed. I tried to smile.

I had tried to call MaryNell on my cell phone on the way, but I couldn't seem to remember her number. Or how to use the phone. Somebody else must have called her, though. I'd lost all sense of time, but at some point she was there. Shaking her head and working really hard at holding the lecture in, saving it for later. A uniformed police officer was visible just outside every time the door opened. And it opened a lot: nurses, aides, checking, peering, patting and reassuring. A doctor came in, asked me a few questions, shone his tiny light into my eyes, asked about the pain.

Sometime during the night – I think it was night. The ER room had no window, Sam came in. A nurse was with him.

'He says he's a friend. Is that true?'

In my current condition I was having trouble answering questions that were a lot simpler than that one. I managed to nod.

'You want him out, he's out, hon.'

Good. I nodded again. That was a mistake.

'We need to talk,' he said.

'Do I need a lawyer?'

The nurse, on her way out, turned at that, but I waved something that she understood to mean that it was OK. She left.

Sam looked over at MaryNell in her neutral corner and nodded. She didn't say anything.

Sam shook his head. 'No. You've got a concussion. We couldn't use anything you said anyway.'

Reassuring.

'I saw the pictures, got the CD,' he said.

I was thinking clearly enough to realize something was wrong with that. 'How?'

'What?'

'How? How'd you get in? You didn't break down my door so it would match my impatiens, did you?'

He shook his head. 'No.' He nodded toward MaryNell.

'MaryNell let me in before she came over here.' There was a glimmer of a grim smile. 'You told me where to find the CD. I didn't try to read your diary.'

I didn't bite.

'Can you tell me about it?' he asked.

'About what?'

'The pictures.'

I could tell he was trying to control his temper. This time, this one time, I couldn't blame him.

The pictures. Of Fly. 'I didn't know.' Just speaking, thinking and making words, was taking a lot of effort. 'I went to Freeport to do a . . . a site inspection, for a group. I just took pictures on the street. I didn't pick up the prints until . . .' What day was it? '. . . yesterday?' Was that possible? Only yesterday? 'No, Monday.' My eyes filled with tears. I couldn't help it. 'I . . . I thought it looked like him. I thought it was him. But, how random is that? I was going to show them to you. I called you. But then you came, and those women were marching, and you were mad. I didn't think about it while you were there. So I went to talk to Marcella. To ask about the day Erika was killed.' My head was throbbing. How could it hurt to think? I pressed my hands against my temples. 'You know about that, but also I wanted to sort of see if I thought she was hiding something. She'd been Fly's secretary for years. I thought if he really was alive, if anyone had helped him, it would probably have been her.'

Sam just listened. And glowered. Made notes in that note-book that was always with him. It wasn't like him to be this restrained. Must be the brain injury.

I took a deep breath and went on. That hurt, too. 'Then, right before I left to go to Marcella's, I got this message.'

'What kind of message?'

'On the computer. An instant message, no name, but it had to be Fly. I can't think now. Exactly what he said, but it was him. It had to be him. And he didn't know what was going on either.'

He didn't explode. I thought he would, and I know he would have if he hadn't thought that would have gotten him thrown out of the ER. The barely controlled anger was scarier. 'You had an email from Franklin Young yesterday?'

I shook my head. Another mistake. 'Sort of. An instant

message. No name. He didn't say much, just enough for me to know who he was, nothing you could prove anything by.'

Sam's face was stony. MaryNell was all but invisible.

A nurse opened the door. 'You OK?' The question was to me, but she gave Sam a sharp look. She looked over at the EKG monitor, and I realized what had brought her in. The line was going crazy. 'If things don't settle down in here, your friends are going to have to leave.'

'I'm OK. Thanks. I need to talk to him.'

She didn't look convinced, but she shut the door.

'He knew what was happening,' I continued. 'I mean, when I got home, he knew about Marcella. I mean, he might have just been to the *Tennessean* website. But Madison seemed glad he was dead. Anyway, Fly knew I had taken his picture in Freeport. He suggested I trade that for information. So that's what I did.'

Mark walked in the room then. He saw Sam and almost backed out, but he came inside and closed the door. He nodded to Sam, then to MaryNell. He went to stand beside her in the corner but didn't say anything.

'I called Mark' – I looked at him – 'and he set up the meeting. The reporter didn't know who'd originally given him the story. So I went to see. Al Evanston met him. I waited until they left, but when I went to my car, it was George Madison who grabbed me.'

'Did he say anything to you?'

I tried to remember. 'No.' A tear that had been threatening trickled down my face. 'Yes. He said it would look like I was drunk, a woman alone downtown. He said something about first Charlie, then Marcella. He . . . he said I was the best travel agent he'd ever had.'

Sam nodded. His face was like stone, hard and set. He closed his little notebook and stood. 'We'll need a complete statement, but that'll have to wait.' He turned to glare at Mark. Mark tried to shrink into the wall. Sam turned back to me. 'OK if I go back in your house, turn on your computer?'

I nodded. Barely. He'd have done it anyway. It would have just taken him a while to get a court order. MaryNell held out her key to my house. Sam left, and I closed my eyes.

SIXTY-FIVE

Do you remember . . .
The touch of my hand . . .
The feel of my lips . . .
Your head on my shoulder . . .
The surf on the sand . . .
Do you remember?

Stick Anderson

They let me go home in the morning. The doctor told me if I played for the Titans, it would be a while before he'd clear me to play. I still felt rotten. My head still hurt. Sam called before I left. He told MaryNell he'd come by my house to get a full statement and that George Madison and Al Evanston were supposed to turn themselves in today.

'He said their lawyers had called,' MaryNell reported. 'No admission. They're coming in because they've heard there are warrants out for them. He said he'd see you later.'

'Was that all?'

'Pretty much. He asked how you were. Something about your head being the safest place for you to be hit. Something to do with it being hard.'

'Oh.'

We pulled into my driveway. The Spider was there. Sam must have had someone bring it home. His daughter Julie was there, too, with MaryNell's daughter Melissa. Planting where my impatiens had bloomed so gloriously last week. They stood as we got out of MaryNell's car, but they seemed afraid to speak.

I walked carefully, trying not to move my head.

'How are you?' Melissa asked in a way that told me just how bad I looked.

'I'm OK. Really. What are you guys doing?'

Julie spoke. 'We saved most of the plants. They'll bloom again, I think. But we planted some new ones in with them. I think we got the right color.'

My eyes filled, and I knew I was about to cry. But I knew that would make my head hurt worse. 'Thanks.'

'Mrs Morgan brought you some soup, and I made you some cookies.' Julie made great chocolate-chip cookies.

I went inside. I needed a shower. But first I turned on my computer. I flipped through the email, nothing I had to deal with now, messages from Barbara, Betty, Pam and Melinda. I'd call them later. Nothing from Fly. I don't know what I expected, but I was disappointed. I left it on.

I lay down, feeling too bad to sleep, too bad to do anything else.

The girls came in quietly when they were finished. I thanked them, but it didn't express how touched I was. I'd have to do something nice for them. Later. When I felt better.

Sometime in the afternoon, Sam and two detectives came. They each had their own little notepads, and one had a tape recorder. I went through my story, answered their questions. Sam said they'd get the statement typed up for me to sign.

MaryNell stayed and took care of me and tried not to hover. It was about seven when Sam knocked at the door again. MaryNell was obviously expecting him. She let him in, asked if I needed anything, gathered up her stuff to go.

'Thanks.' I seemed to be saying that a lot. She waved it away. 'No. I mean it. Thanks. And thanks for the flowers. Having the girls replant them. I know that was your idea. That was sweet.'

'It wasn't my idea,' she said. 'It was Sam's.' And she left.

'Any more messages?' Sam asked.

'No.'

He nodded. 'We'll probably have to get a computer expert to take a look at your computer. See if we can trace the messages. Trace the IP address.' He was matter of fact. No accusation. No apologies. 'It's probably going to be some Internet café, someplace very public and anonymous.'

I walked back into the room where the computer was. A message blinked. I might as well call Sam to see it.

'Sam!' Ahhh. Too loud.

Sam came and stood behind me.

The message said:

Sorry. You OK? For the record, I never took any HealthwaRx funds. I don't plan to come home and defend myself, but I wanted you to know. My guess is Al and George had been messing with the money, and Charlie noticed something. I was beginning to suspect something myself. And I guess they decided my death was a good opportunity to withdraw a bonus. Your detective friend should be able to track that down.

I don't know what I would have responded if I'd been alone. A little innocent fraud? But three people were dead, and two children had nothing but very large trust funds.

I looked at Sam. 'You could ask where he is,' Sam said.

I could. I wasn't trying to protect him, but I didn't like being used to track him. I shrugged.

Where are you?

I wouldn't do that to you, make you an accessory after the suspicion. 😬

What about your kids?

You don't think my mother will be better for them than Erika and I were?

He had a point. Cowardly, irresponsible and self-serving, but a point. I had nothing to say to that. One more message appeared.

I never meant to get you involved in this. Bad timing once again. Goodbye.

I turned to Sam. He was watching me.

'We'll be trying to track him down,' he said.

'I know.'

We stood there, looking at each other.

Finally Sam spoke. 'I need to know how much that matters to you.'

I didn't know how to put that into a twenty-five-words-or-less answer. Especially not with a concussion. I couldn't say it didn't matter. Fly was a friend. Sort of. And he was my first love. But what he'd done was illegal, not to mention that it had hurt a lot of people. I had seen his mother's face. And I wasn't still in love with him. And this man had talked two teenagers into planting flowers in my yard.

'It may take me a while to answer that.'

'I've got all night. You don't need to be left alone. I'm taking this shift.'

'I have a head injury. I can't be held responsible for anything I say or do.'

He snorted. Then he pushed a strand of hair off my face. 'Yeah, you might do something crazy, like go out in the middle of the night to meet a murderer.'

'Oh, Sam.'

Then he put his arms around me.

SIXTY-SIX

I didn't get any more messages from Fly, and, so far at least, the police haven't found him. They may not have tried too hard. No insurance claims had been filed, and he hadn't had anything to do with the murders. That had been all Al and George. Auditors were still working through the records, but apparently Charles Patton had found accounting irregularities. Al's and George's attorneys were still trying to bargain on that one. Erika wanted them to buy her out. She demanded twice the highest price per share the stock had ever reached. Apparently she suspected from the beginning that they, not Fly, had embezzled the funds and that Charlie's murder wasn't so random, and she threatened to call for a Securities and Exchange Commission investigation unless they paid her. Marcella knew they'd met with Erika. Erika's caller ID showed that Marcella had called her less than an hour before I had found her. So Marcella had to go, too. Al Evanston knew what medication to give Marcella and how much would be too much. The wine was insurance. What the ME hadn't said publicly right away was that bruises indicated a struggle. And I was just a little too late.

Captain Dave called to tell me that the *Manana* had been sold. A boat broker out of Nassau had made a cash offer for the boat, sight unseen, which Fly's estate had been glad to accept. The broker had hired a charter captain to ferry the *Manana* to Georgetown, Grand Cayman, after it was refitted. Captain Dave didn't know the new owner's name.

In that late summer and early fall, my impatiens were the most beautiful they'd ever been. I was beginning to believe that last love might be as special as first love.

I was in a bar on Cayman Brac a year or so later. I'd taken a day trip over from Georgetown to escape the cruise ship crowds shopping on Grand Cayman. The sun was brilliant, and I was blinded when I walked into the relatively cool gloom. Just a few people were in the dim room. I went to the bar and ordered a club soda. Twists of lemon and lime. And ice, lots of ice. When the bartender brought it over, he set it on a napkin with writing. 'Gentleman in the corner.' He nodded toward the far side of the bar, then said, 'Blimey. He seems to've gone. Cold feet.' He grinned and shrugged.

'It wasn't "Whiter Shade of Pale",' the note read. 'It was "Unchained Melody".'

I remember when we were eighteen
Everything was out there and waiting
On the top of our world,
our very small world
We'd found everything that mattered
You and me, when we were eighteen

Stick Anderson

ACKNOWLEDGMENTS

Thank you to David and the Lady Skyhawks, Julie Schoerke Gallagher, Smyrna High School Class of 1970, Us Five, Hank and Margaret Dye for the renewed Spider, Ronnie and Priscilla Thweatt and Charlie and Charlotte Self for sailing, Mark, Howard, still the best neighbor in the world, and to Rachel, Martin, Natasha, Tess, Aneesha and the wonderful crew at Severn House and Canongate.